THE KING'S KINDNESS

SARAH FENLON FALK

For all the children who long for a family.
You are precious. You are loved.

Cover design by Cheriefox.com
Interior design by Sarah Fenlon Falk

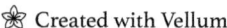 Created with Vellum

THANK YOU FOR READING
THE SAGE CHEVAL SERIES

If you're new to the series,
here's where to start:

The Servant Prince, Book One
The Melancholy Princess, Book Two
The Guardian's Gift, Book Three
The Path of Endurance, Book Four

INTRODUCTION

Found in ancient Scripture:
"Let your kindness be known to all people."
Philippians 4:5

Kingdom of Monde, Decree of Succession:
"At such a time, by act of God or accident,
the throne of Monde be vacant,
The eldest son of the afore-reigning king
shall then be crowned.
In order for this prince to reign,
he must be fifteen years of age,
Unless circumstance requires a king and
this prince, while less than reigning age, proves capable."

PROLOGUE

"What is it?"

"I don't know. I can't see it very well..."

The young woman squinted hard into the setting sun. She put a hand up to shield her eyes for a better look and stared hard at the object floating on the water not far from shore. At first, Luca had thought it was a branch, but the closer it came to shore the more confused she became by the object. She wasn't sure what she was seeing. Whatever it was, it was being brought in by the waves that had been so brutal all day long and were only now settling with the waning sun.

"Should we go out for it?"

Gavin had seen the floating object from high in the trees. He had been gathering what fruit had clung to them, that which the recent storm had left behind. It had been a harsh day at sea, which had made it hard on their village, difficult on their people. They had tied down all they could and had huddled together against the wind. The storm had rushed over the tiny island of Labri and had stopped almost as quickly as it had come. It was not the worst storm they had ever seen, it had taken no lives from the islanders that day. The most severe storms always threatened to take a life.

Luca had lost neighbors, friends, people she had loved. That is how she came to be the surrogate mother for three of the children on the island. They were not of her flesh and blood but they were the children of her heart now. Gavin was one of hers.

"I think we should wait. The waves seem to be bringing it to us," Luca spoke, putting a gentle hand on her son's shoulder.

The waves continued to rage and seemed to fight against the wind, crashing into one another. Luca knew if there had been a boat out in this weather it most certainly would have been lost. Perhaps whatever was floating toward them now was leftover from a shipwreck.

Luca had lived on the island all her life and she knew the sea well enough to understand it's temperament. This had been an angry day. It was no wonder that the sea had dug something up or wrecked something, anything that dared to cross it, and now it was dragging this very thing to the island, to her.

With the sun a bit lower and the object a bit closer, Luca could see that it was indeed a large piece of drifting wood. But it was no branch, it was wood from the side of a ship, and on it a person seemed to be clinging. The figure moved an arm, a movement that proved the body's limbs were as limp as a dead fish. Luca could see it was a man and she could also tell he was in trouble.

Luca and Gavin jumped into action at the sight of that smallest of movements. Luca pulled the bottom hem of her skirt up into a knot around her waist so that she could wade out into the water without its hindrance. She pulled her long dark hair up as well. She was already waist deep in the water and she could see the man's bearded, weathered face. Gavin was by her side, wading out into the churning water.

The man's clothing was tattered and there were several wounds visible on his arms and neck. He was unconscious. Before the water was over their heads, Luca and Gavin had reached the man and grabbed hold of the wood he was floating on. They swam alongside the makeshift raft, guiding it to shore. The sea relinquished its victim more easily than Luca would have thought, and soon they were pulling the driftwood, then the man, onto the sandy shore.

Together they rolled the large man off the makeshift raft and onto the sand, putting him on his back. Luca lay her head on his chest and could hear his heart beating within, however weakly. She felt his forehead then his hands. On his left hand was a large gold ring with an "R" carved into it. The R was surrounded by rubies with 4 emeralds marking top, bottom and each side.

This man must be rich, very important or both, Luca thought.

Brushing the thought aside she continued to search him for signs of wounds. His body was cold but his forehead was hot. He had a fever, perhaps an infection from his wounds. If he had been in a ship wreck she was sure that it was possible that he had more wounds than could be seen. They needed to get him back to the village, back to her hut where she could better care for him.

She looked toward the tree line. No one could be seen coming from or going to the village. Luca imagined she and Gavin could get the man back to her hut, they just needed to figure out how.

"Quick! Help me," Luca instructed, gather up a few large branches to tie together as a mat on which to put the man.

When they tried to move him onto the mat they had constructed, the man moaned.

"Shh, now," Luca reassured him with a soft hand to his cheek. "We will care for you."

Together, Gavin and Luca rolled the man onto the mat, grabbed a hold of the thick part of the branches, and pulled, leaving a deep track in the sand as they made their way up the bank and into the forest. The grass and foliage was almost as difficult to pull the man through as the sand had been. Soon they found their way into the clearing where their village was situated. Mercifully, Luca's hut was not far and soon the man was carefully positioned by the fire and his wet clothing was being removed.

When they rolled him over he groaned and held his side. His left side was badly bruised and it was clear at least two of his ribs had been broken.

Luca created a poultice of seaweed and lay it gently on his bruises then bound it to him with cloth that she wrapped around him. She lay a cool wet cloth on his forehead to help reduce the fever. Then covered him with the few blankets she possessed and left him to rest. She knew he would need food and clean water to drink as soon as he was coherent enough to consume it so she set about making a hot soup. Once this was gently simmering over the fire she left to fetch clean water.

When she returned she noticed the man's eyes were open. He tried to move when he saw her enter the tent but she shushed him again and lay two gentle hands on his shoulders.

"You must not move," she said.

He understood what she said but looked at her questioningly as she spoke with an accent he did not recognize. As confused as he was, he obeyed her and lay back down.

She brought water in a cup and lifted his head with her free hand. He sipped the water. It was refreshing and he grasped the cup with both of his hands to force it back to his lips.

"Slowly," she advised.

He nodded and obeyed.

She then took the cup and filled it with the soup she had prepared. She knelt next to him, blowing into the bowl so the liquid would not burn him. She tested it and when it was just right for her patient, she lifted his head once again and poured the broth between his cracked lips.

Again, he was eager to receive it and she had to remind him to take his time.

He paused, looking into her dark eyes and nodding his consent to do it her way. She nodded back at him in agreement. He raised one of his hands and placed it on top of her hand. Together they held the cup. He raised it to his lips to drink slowly.

When he was done, she smiled down at him again and noticed his green eyes looked a bit more lively now.

Through his overgrown beard and mustache she could see he was trying to smile at her too.

1

"We must have a king!" Sir Edward argued his point in a voice more stern than Prince William ever remembered hearing from him. "This is a turbulent time! If that faction of Oblager youth turn any more of their clan to join their cause we must show them they are a mere gang of rebels coming up against a firm and steady kingdom and we can only do that with a king who is present to rule his kingdom!"

"Intimidation alone is not going to shake their resolve, Edward," Sir Francis argued.

Princess Margaret was amazed at how Sir Francis was able to keep his cool even in the midst of a dispute. She sat between the two men, her eyebrows raised in realization that she had never heard the two argue in such a way before.

"It is not within the law to crown Prince Robert king until his fifteenth birthday. Not only that, we are still uncertain as to our dear King Elyon's whereabouts. Until we receive word from the Kingdom of Estrea confirming his death in battle we cannot in good conscience put his son on the throne!"

"I know the law, *Francis*," Sir Edward countered, using Sir Francis's name as if it were an expletive. "However, these are extraordinary circumstances and our laws provide for extraordinary circumstances. Do remember that the Decree of Succession also states that if a king is missing from his throne for any reason, after one year gone he may be replaced, in service of the kingdom and in care of his people! We are swiftly approaching one full year since our own king was known to be alive..."

This last statement served to diffuse the conversation a bit and everyone in the throne room was quiet now, lost in thoughts of their missing king.

Prince William and Princess Margaret sat on their own thrones looking from one of their father's wise men, the Doyen, to the other as if watching some sort of ball game.

The thrones of the oldest four children of the House of Rosh sat vacant. The Oblager had taken Lillian, stolen her off the back of her trusted Sage Cheval, Temperance, the night before. Instead of putting their heads together to strategize ways to get the princess back the Doyen had entered the castle gates at the first light of dawn already arguing about crowning fourteen-year-old Prince Robert. It was just two months before the prince would turn fifteen and could legally be crowned king.

Prince William tried not to think about it though he couldn't help but consider how this would impact *his* birthday celebration, which under normal circumstances would be held just days from now. As soon as the thought popped into his head he reprimanded himself and dismissed it. He could not, and would not concern himself with thoughts of a birthday celebration when his poor sister was most likely cold and afraid aboard that awful Oblager ship still moored in Falaise Bay.

He looked over at Lady Susan who was staring blankly at the floor, a pained look still wrinkling her forehead. She had returned to the castle before the first light, before the Doyen had arrived, and had been too shocked to fully tell the story of what had happened on the road. Lady Claire had tried her best to soothe her friend, but to no avail.

Now they were all gathered in the throne room with a fire blazing in the hearth. The sun had fully risen and the smell of the midday meal was in the air. Margaret only noticed because she was hungry. It had been a very long morning and while it had been extremely emotional, emotions never trumped basic instinct for her. Even when she had felt so sad those many weeks, losing sleep due to vivid dreams and a rush of memories of her mother who had died when Margaret was only three years old, even then she had taken time to eat. When she felt down she preferred solitude and would eat by herself in those times, but she had never abandoned herself to suffer hunger.

William shifted in his seat.

Sir Francis broke the silence, "I advise we wait. Let us send out another dove-"

He was cut off by a scoffing noise made by his fellow Doyen.

"Bah!" Sir Edward cut in, "*Another* dove? Do you know how many doves we have sent in search of King Elyon? I would not even venture to guess at this point - too many to count!"

"Send another dove and if it does not return within a week's time..." Sir Francis continued, then paused, running a hand over his mouth and over the scruff on his chin before saying, "We will crown Prince Robert king of Monde."

Sir Edward looked at him, clearly surprised, Margaret thought. He nodded in agreement.

"What is to be done about Princess Lillian? Isn't *that* the most pressing matter?" Prince William spoke loudly, rising from his throne. "Why aren't we focusing on a strategy for her rescue?"

"Yes, your highness, it is most pressing," Sir Edward responded, "but as we have said, Prince Robert and his guard are working to devise a strategy to retrieve her."

Prince William just nodded and rested his head on his hand, propped up on the side of his throne. He realized he was very tired, weary really, and decided he would need to get to bed early, if he would be able to sleep at all. He jumped up to jolt himself awake and announced, "I'm going to send that dove now."

Princess Margaret sat up straighter in her throne and looked around the room. She wanted something to do too. She stood up and announced her plans, "And I am going to Colline to check on the finishes for the house."

She walked toward the entrance to the throne room, stopped short as the warm, thick smells of a meal being prepared reached her. "I'll go after lunch," she added, then she was gone.

Lady Susan hadn't budged. Until today, she had been very interested to know how the house on the side of the hill near Colline was progressing but that was before Princess Lillian had been taken right before her very eyes. She had powerless to stop it. Now she couldn't bring herself to move, couldn't allow herself to enjoy anything until Princess Lillian was recovered from the grip of the Oblager.

Sir Francis walked over to her, she sat frozen near the entrance to the throne room. He gently touched her shoulder and as if he had the power to read a mind said,

"You are not to blame for Princess Lillian's capture, Lady Susan. No one holds you responsible."

A tear slid down the lady's cheek. Slowly she looked up at Sir Francis without looking him in the eye.

"I do," she said.

"Madam, your wisdom and skills are needed now, more than ever! Please do not hold yourself so harshly in contempt. Do not remain closed off for long. We require your presence in this matter."

When the room was still and quiet Lady Susan finally stood, took a deep breath in, raised herself to stand even taller, lifted her chin and resolved to do anything she could to get the princess back. She would use every ounce of her will to stop dwelling on the memory that replayed over and over in her mind of the small band of Oblager who had ridden away with the princess in the dark of night. She had watched them disappear into darkness, but soon, she decided, no matter what she would have to do to see it done, she *would* watch her princess ride through the gates of Castle Grange once again.

2

The wind off the waves of the Beaumere Sea blew up the cliffs at the port of Falaise Bay and stung the faces of the young men standing there. The Captain of the Guard, Sir Logan, stood next to his princes Theodore and Robert. Flanking the other side of the young royal men was Elijah, a soldier who had served in the king's guard and who had more recently been asked to work closely with Sir Logan as his right hand man.

Prince Theodore used his bulky sleeve to wipe away the pellets of frosty rain that had smacked his cheeks and left them red.

They were looking out into the bay where the remaining ships of the Oblager were now anchored. Erik, the young and rebellious Oblager had taken his ships away from the safety of the docks in port during the night and were now anchored at the mouth of Falaise Bay. It seemed an odd move, to leave the safety of the port and sail out into the bay only to anchor there. Winter was coming and the open sea would not be safe for much longer.

"What are we waiting for?" Prince Theodore said. "If they're not going to sail away let's go get them!"

"It's not that easy!" Robert responded to his brother with a snap. He felt as if they'd been over this a hundred times in the last several hours. "If they have Lillian on one of their ships we can't just go off sinking those ships!"

Theodore looked at Robert with shock on his face. Had Robert read his mind? He had thought that exact thing: sink their ships. But, that was before his sister Lillian was aboard one of them.

He softened and let out a deep breath. "You're absolutely right," he agreed. "I just want to *do* something. I can't stand sitting still."

"We *are* doing something, Your Grace," Sir Logan encouraged the young prince. "And remember your sister is not alone out there. Malaya is on one of those ships as well. No doubt she is keeping an eye on the princess."

"Let us hope," Prince Theodore said with a nod.

After several moments of silently staring at the ships being tossed about by the waves below them, Theodore whispered, "What are you doing?"

Robert knew it would be difficult for his brother to stay put, but their next move was uncertain and unclear. Until something was decided among his wise men and captain of his guard, the young prince knew it was important not to jump into anything.

Sir Logan stood keeping an eye on Prince Theodore. He could feel the tension and frustration of the energetic young man. They would have to come up with a plan to either attack or defend against the Oblager sooner rather than later. The tension was getting to be too much for the prince.

"Sir Logan, should we go and run drills with the men?"

Elijah suggested, as if he too could read minds and had read the mind of his captain.

"Yes," Sir Logan agreed. "Prince Theodore, will you be overseeing? Would you like to inspect the men, the weapons?"

Prince Theodore nodded and followed behind the men as they retreated away from the cliffs to the camp.

Prince Robert called to one of his guards.

"I'd like you to take a couple of men and head to the cave. Be certain our ships are ready to sail."

"Yes, my prince," the man bowed then ran to do as he had been instructed. Prince Robert turned to watch the tumultuous scene below. It wouldn't be long before the first snow would fall. The rain was already turning to sleet and soon it would solidify into sparkling white flakes. He determined he would see his sister's face before that day. Before the first snowfall, Lillian would be safe.

He thought about Samuel off on a mission to seek support from the kingdom to their south. He prayed King Facile and Allia would agree to be their ally and would send ships soon. If there was a battle at sea, they would need those ships. Until they were certain of aid from Allia, Robert knew their own ships needed to be tended to. They were weakest when challenged at sea. This was nothing new. On land they not only had men from the villages as well as trained soldiers, but they also had the Sage Cheval. They had beaten the Oblager together before. He hoped they could do it again.

Prince Robert made his way to the white tent where they had met with the Oblager to try to agree upon peace, what seemed like just hours ago.

Lady Dori was standing in the corner of the tent looking out into the bay under the shelter of the canvas.

She had a young guard by her side, likely assigned to her by Elijah.

Prince Robert realized he had not seen her eat in a while and asked her about it.

"I am not hungry, Your Grace," she said. "I admit, concern has stolen my appetite."

She sat down and sighed. She had tried to bring peace to a volatile situation when the Oblager, a wayfaring people who threatened to scavenge their land, had appeared on their shores. Now she couldn't believe what was happening. They had taken Princess Lillian captive on one of their ships. Lady Dori tried to think what else she could have done differently to try to bring about peace. The options had been limited with the younger Oblager shouting for preservation of the "old ways", wanting to take whatever they needed, to pillage the Kingdom of Monde, while the elder Oblager seemed tired and worn, relieved at the prospect of being gifted a land they could call home. But they had all gone round and round until at last, Erik, the younger Oblager, had rebelled against his own leader and forced a shift in discussion. Silas, the elder Oblager, had taken his family and the people still loyal to him and all were now safely on the Isle of Drepos, preparing to live out their days in the beauty of the garden island surrounded by the magnificent Beaumere Sea. Yes, they were safe, but Princess Lillian...

"You must not blame yourself for the situation we are in," Prince Robert said, having joined her in her silent contemplation.

He reached over and stoked the fire with a stick, then rubbed his hands together in front of the growing flames to warm them.

"It is a wonder that we have not had to face such difficulty before now, given that my father has been gone nearly two years. So much *could* have happened in that time."

"So much *has* happened in the last several months, Your Grace," Lady Dori asserted. She didn't want to argue with him, but did want to give credit where credit was due. Their kingdom had been through many trials in very recent times: plague, grief, celebrations and now the Oblager at their shores. Any of these things would be much for a young prince to handle and even Lady Dori herself was beginning to feel the weight of it.

"You have carried the burden well, Prince Robert," she acknowledged with a bow.

The young prince was thankful he wasn't the only one who thought it had been a rough few months though he wasn't sure how well he had handled anything. There were still enemy ships in his port, his sister was captive aboard one of them, his father was nowhere to be found and he felt most moments he was simply trying to keep from shaking with fear. But he thanked her nonetheless.

"I appreciate your support, Lady Dori. I know how hard you have worked and all you have sacrificed to try to bring this peace about. It is unfortunate that not every one of the Oblager were able to accept the peace offered to them. Who would have thought Erik would have gone to such an extreme as to take..." his voice trailed off as if he couldn't make himself say the words, "so extreme as to take the princess..."

Lady Dori placed a gentle hand on his arm but remained silent.

Prince Robert smiled at her. Then set his jaw, quickly turning his mind to the business at hand.

"Lady Dori," he spoke gently. "I have a task for you. Do you feel strong enough to ride?"

She nodded, "Yes, my prince."

"Well then, I need you to return to the castle. The Doyen must understand that despite what they feel is necessary at this time I will not leave this post until all is settled between the Oblager and I."

She nodded in agreement.

"While we are but two months and a few days from my fifteenth birthday, Sir Edward has already told me he believes I should be crowned king as soon as possible. I need for you to tell him if things have not settled... That is, if we are forced into battle with Oblager... If we must go..." he had a hard time finding the right words. His mind whirred with all the possibilities of what could happen in the coming days. All of the victories that could be won and all the potential losses. "I will oblige them and receive the crown as soon as the Doyen feel it is necessary to secure the kingdom."

Lady Dori, who had stood by patiently, waiting for her prince to find the words, bowed to him obediently. As she turned to go Prince Robert nodded at the young guard who had been standing near to her. The guard bowed, understanding the prince's command for him to accompany the lady. He obeyed immediately.

3

The crew aboard the ship Freedom had been set to menial tasks for days. While the princess was kept below deck for the most part, the men were working on deck to tidy the ship and prepare it for voyage. The brief periods that Princess Lillian was allowed outside of the captain's cabin she was able to observe the state of the ship. It was indeed a sturdy craft and one that had seen its fair share of rough weather at sea. This did not comfort her however and she always looked for Malaya when possible. She hadn't seen her since that first night. It did give her hope to know that Malaya was planning their escape but she would rather have had the comfort of the girl's presence.

Princess Lillian's meals were brought to her by the same men each time. That didn't matter to her except that she was thankful to see the same kind young man and thankful that the rough, angry sailor didn't come alone. Should the gruff man ever come alone, or without his protagonist, Lillian wasn't sure how their visits would go. She was always sure to give the kind young man the courtesy of eye contact and a polite smile or nod. She didn't want to seem ungrateful. She would take any kindness where she could get it.

Princess Lillian was allowed out on deck for a walk twice that day and was able to breathe in some fresh air. While the weather was certainly colder than the blue sky and sunshine would suggest, Lillian appreciated not only the ability to stretch her legs, but also to have clear sight of the port town at Falaise Bay and further up the hill to the white tent where she knew her brothers were. She could only imagine what they were going through, planning a way to get her back. If the water wasn't so frigid or the waves so tumultuous, she felt she could jump overboard and swim to them now. Had it only been two days since she'd been with them?

Lillian stopped mid stride along the deck and hugged her shawl to her chest. Squinting in the midday sun she looked up at the big white tent high on the hill and imagined she could see her brothers looking down at her. Her heart ached just to be with them.

"Oh, Margaret," Lillian sighed under her breath, imagining what her younger sister must have gone through when Lady Susan arrived at the castle without her. The lady would have returned only with the stories of an attack under cover of darkness and how the Oblager had stolen Margaret's sister away.

Lillian brushed a tear from her cheek and continued her circle around the deck. For the most part the crew worked around her, behaving as if she weren't even there until at last Erik barked the order for her to be returned to her cabin and two of the crew members led her back to her room.

Princess Lillian felt as though she had spent a lifetime

on this cold and creaking ship. The Oblager, or the younger crew of Oblager who had rebelled against their own leader, had taken her in the night when there was no one but Lady Susan to protect her. Lady Susan and Temperance. She remembered Temperance, her Cheval, had tried to catch up to the group, had tried to stay with them. But Temperance must have known, Lady Susan must have known, that their best chance at getting her back was to go and tell Prince Robert. He had command of the guards and could send someone to rescue her.

Two long and lonely nights she had waited and hoped for rescue, but it had not come. Now Lillian stood in her cabin with her cloak hugged around her tightly. It seemed the temperature was dropping several degrees by the minute. Winter was quickly approaching and she did not wish for it. That brutal season was made more brutal when experienced on the water. She wondered if Erik, the young Oblager rebel leader, would decide to sail away with her or if there would be an all-out war against her kingdom, against Monde. A shiver ran down her back and caused her whole body to shudder. She took a deep breath and pulled the neck of her cloak up closer to her ears then looked back at the bed. She had been given an extra blanket for her second night and had been warm beneath the wool covers. She was tempted to get back under them now, but resolved to stay up and stay alert.

Malaya was somewhere on this ship and was working to find a way to save her. If her brothers could do nothing from up on the cliff overlooking Falaise Bay then perhaps the young woman, the spy aboard the Freedom, would do it.

Lillian couldn't help but smile, imagining Malaya brandishing a sword and challenging Erik to a duel. While

Lillian couldn't imagine herself being so brave or so strong, it seemed these things came naturally to the young spy. Her throat tickled her and she coughed.

This drafty ship is not a good place to be expected to live out the winter, she thought then shrugged it off. She had every confidence that she would be saved before the first snowfall, one way or another.

~

"Where is that rotten ship," Erik barked at one of his men as they stood on deck with the wind and rain pounding against them.

The man cowered and said nothing.

"They were supposed to be here by now, that was the plan. We need them. How can we go ashore and start raiding the villages until we have a place to put our plunder?"

"Would you like me to send a dove?" The man asked, trying to be helpful.

"No, I don't want you to send a dove! If they're that far away where doves are required, then they are too far! We might as well sail away now and save ourselves the trouble."

The man nodded and left as soon as he was dismissed by a wave of Erik's hand.

"Fool," Erik mumbled under his breath.

He looked out at the dark ocean that was becoming more and more tumultuous as the days went by. The waves grew taller and the winds grew stronger. Erik thought about the young princess below and her brothers standing up on the ridge high above the bay, watching. He had never expected to be sitting here for this long. He had intended to strike quickly and then be gone. His anger grew as he considered this delay.

Perhaps taking the princess was a mistake after all. But there was no turning back now, he knew. He had to stay the course.

4

Before going to the dovecote as had been his intention since breakfast, Prince William waited for the Doyen to return to their study. He had wanted to go out and send a message presently after their discussion in the throne room but he needed to talk with the men privately.

The idea, the very thought that his father *might* be dead was difficult enough to bear, but Sir Francis and Sir Edward wanted to carry on as though King Elyon were already and most certainly dead. To crown Prince Robert the King of Monde would be the same as verifying a death they knew nothing of. This seemed audacious to the youngest prince and he needed to talk to the men about this.

It wasn't long before Prince William could hear the men's voices coming up the stairs. It seemed they were heavily debating something but as soon as they opened the door and saw the young prince standing there they dropped their conversation and bowed.

"Prince William, how may we be of service?" Sir Francis asked.

The young prince waited until the men were behind their desks before he sat. They sat too. Then the boy leaned forward, elbows on knees and said, "I don't understand why you would crown Robert king when my father should be home soon."

The two men looked at one another, a quizzical look, as if asking 'Wasn't he just in the throne room for that discussion?'

Without giving them a chance to answer, Prince William continued. "I don't understand why the focus isn't on strategy for recovering my sister and getting rid of the enemy ships in our bay." The young prince's words became louder with each sentence. "And I am growing *quite* impatient for something to get done! I must see something good happen! What do you have to say about that?"

Before his voice had risen to a full-out shout he pulled himself back into the chair and snapped his mouth shut. He shrugged at the men. His shoulders raised again as he heaved a sigh, exhaling loudly.

"I don't know why I said all that," he said, unable to explain himself further.

After a few more moments of silence Sir Edward leaned across the desk toward his young prince, looking him in the eye.

"Your Grace, it gives us no pleasure to either believe your father to be dead nor to surpass his authority as he may be lost and alive somewhere in this world. Either way we face the necessity of crowning Prince Robert king. We love and are loyal to King Elyon. However, we must tend to the matters at hand. We are most likely headed to war, and an army needs a Commander."

"If there were an easy answer, we would use it," Sir Francis spoke softly. "The good news for our beloved

Princess Lillian is that Malaya is aboard the Oblager ships and will most certainly be able to keep an eye on her. She is as safe as she can be at the moment. And so our focus must be on the greater good, on the Kingdom of Monde and that is why we are talking about crowning your brother before the lawful time, duty may require it."

Prince William sat still, breathing heavily. He wasn't soothed yet.

"There are no quick answers here," Sir Francis finished.

The young prince nodded, speechless.

"I want to give you something," Sir Francis said, getting up from his chair and going over to the smallest bookshelf in the room, situated under one of the windows. From it he removed a book with a dark brown cover. It was a slim book and Prince William could smell the leather of the cover as soon as the book was placed in his hands. He held it to his nose and inhaled again. The smell reminded him of the outdoors. It reminded him of his father.

"It is a book of thoughtful poems, prayers if you will. You may find them encouraging."

"Thank you," Prince William said and rose from his chair. "Thank you both, for your time and your service."

The men rose from their seats and bowed.

With the leather volume clutched in one arm, Prince William quietly closed the door to the Doyen's study behind him. He turned and opened the book to the middle. The book groaned with the work of stretching and bending that had not been imposed upon it for some time. William read the first thing he turned to, then he read it again.

Tucking the book in his jacket he hurried down the stairs. He was ready to be at the dovecote. He did not take his time getting there and ran down the stairs, out of the castle and across the courtyard. He liked his task of caring for the cooing birds of the castle in their tiny stone dwelling. The dovecote was set near the back of the castle walls in the center of one of Grange's many gardens. He enjoyed hearing the low, soft sound of the birds as he approached the place, and appreciated the bit of warmth he felt as he entered through the small arched doorway. He didn't mind the dank, sometimes stale smell of the air, the smell that comes when many birds are living in one place. It was somehow comforting to him. All of it natural and organic. He couldn't explain why he felt so warm and safe here but he felt it all the same.

Once inside, he paused at the small stand at the center of the structure. He bowed his head in prayer as he stood with his hands on the table, a small piece of paper in one hand, his writing tool in the other.

"Father," he whispered, head still bowed, "Please, Father. Come home."

Then he stood and quickly wrote a note, again beseeching his father to come home and adding: "Lillian has been taken" and "We need you."

He wanted to tell his father all of the reasons why they needed him, all of the reasons he should return now. He wanted to demand that his father come and prove to everyone that he was not dead. But, there was no room for all of that in a note and there was no time to compose it.

William quickly rolled the scroll, skillfully tying it with twine from the spool at the edge of the stand. From the leather pouch hanging off the side he drew out a handful of seed and laid it on the stand. Soon two doves were on the perch and pecking at the treat William had provided them. William kissed the scroll then tied the message to the leg of one of the doves who had approached him. He held the bird gently in both of his hands and facing the window to the east, the window opening toward Estrea, he tossed the dove upward and it took flight, flying out the window high above the young prince's head. He stood looking up long after the bird had disappeared. He was still praying. This had to work. Not only because Lillian needed rescuing but also because if their father did not return soon and Robert was crowned king, it would make their father's death seem like more of a reality. William could put no words to that kind of feeling either.

He dropped his head then looked at the second dove that had come to the stand. The bird pecked at its food as William was lost in thought. He thought about Lillian. He thought about Samuel and wondered where he was on his journey to Allia. What was he doing? *How* was he doing? Would Allia be welcoming? Would they agree to send ships and help the Kingdom of Monde? Would King Facile do what they all hoped he would?

William picked up another small piece of paper and pulled out the book Sir Francis had given him. He opened it dead-center and found what he had read earlier, then began to write:

Listen to the whisper
    Hope on the wind.
    Trust not what you see or feel,
    Find truth within.
    Hold fast,
    Stay strong,
    Wait.
    What you seek,
    What is true,
    Your grace will

Bring to you.

He wasn't sure what it all meant yet, but William had found comfort in the words, inspiration even, and he wanted to share them with Samuel. Again, he rolled the scroll and tied it with twine. He looked at the fat dove sitting before him and he smiled. Tying the scroll to the bird, he picked it up and held it in both of his hands. This time he approached the window facing south and lifted the bird gently into the air. The dove flapped his wings with great force and seemed suspended in place for a time. Then, once he found the fortitude, the dove lifted and was soon gone through the window toward Allia.

5

P rincess Margaret didn't have to ask twice. Lady Susan knew it would do her no good to argue with the youngest of her charges, so when Princess Margaret had said Lady Susan should come with her to Colline, she had immediately agreed. Even though she felt she should avoid any of the happenings at the castle or in the kingdom since she had been the one to lose Princess Lillian to the Oblager. Nevertheless, she knew arguing with Princess Margaret was never an option, the young princess would always win out in the end.

And so it was that very afternoon, she found herself with the youngest princess, out in the stables. It had been a while since Lady Susan had spent time with Solicitude, the Sage Cheval who had chosen her years ago. Now here they were, Princess Margaret and herself, packing up Delight and Solicitude for a ride out to Colline.

There were a number of the Sage Cheval, the oldest and wisest of horse breeds in the world, who had chosen to live at the castle and bond themselves to the royal family. The majority of the Sage Cheval however, still lived in the North

Country, free from the burden and risk of caring for and loving a human. Delight had chosen this young princess to be hers when Margaret was just a baby. They were both adventurous and liked to move fast, though Delight found she had to remind her girl to slow down from time to time, to keep her from trouble.

"I think it is the perfect use of that beautiful cottage," Margaret had confided in her Cheval.

"It is a fine idea," Delight had admitted upon hearing that her girl wanted to use the restored cottage as a respite house for soldiers recovering from injuries of war. While war had not officially been declared, preparations were being made throughout the kingdom, in the event that it became inevitable.

"It's such a beautiful spot and the fireplace in the main room will keep it nice and warm through the winter months. I hope there will be little need of it, but in the event any of our soldiers are wounded in battle and need a place to recover, this would be perfect."

Princess Margaret had found the cottage at a time when she needed it most and hoped that the men who would potentially be putting themselves in harm's way or who might be harmed for the kingdom's cause, would find comfort and healing there just as she had.

"It is a lovely idea," Lady Susan agreed as Princess Margaret reiterated her plan to the woman as they rode out of the castle gates and toward the villages.

There was a wet chill in the air and Lady Susan knew this meant it would not be long before the first snowflake fell.

"Should Prince Samuel succeed and Allia send us the ships we require, perhaps there will be no need for war and therefore no need to use the cottage in such a way."

Princess Margaret said, "We shall cross that bridge when or if we come to it. But until then, it will be good to have the cabin ready."

The day had indeed turned cold but it didn't slow the Cheval a bit and it didn't take long for them to make their way through the woods, past the village of Valea in the valley beside them. They watched for a moment as the people below busied themselves with preparations for the midday meal. They continued on and soon they were climbing up into the hills near the village of Colline.

Margaret felt herself warm, her muscles relax and soften, as they entered the small grove of trees that sheltered the little cottage. She loved this place. It had been the place where memories of her mother had first returned to her. She had once believed she couldn't remember her mother at all. Most three-year-olds don't hold onto images or recollect events, instead, they keep feelings and impressions. But she had memories. She could remember her mother's long, dark hair, much like her own. At moments she could even remember the sound of Queen Amalia's voice, her laugh. Even now. Margaret smiled as tears stung her eyes. She squinted to chase them away and with a deep breath said to her companion, "I miss her, Delight."

"As do I." Delight had known Queen Amalia for some time before the young princess had been born and the young Cheval would never forget her humor and her sensitivity. "Your mother was one of a kind. As are you."

Princess Margaret smiled.

They arrived at the cottage before mid-morning and Princess Margaret was prepared to get to work right away. She led Lady Susan through the house explaining her vision for where beds would be placed, food trays, work stations. Lady Susan made suggestions as to where she might grow her medicinal plants and store her oils.

"You've done a lot of work here, Princess! I'm not sure there's much left to be done other than accommodating for the potential patients we may have."

"You are right," Princess Margaret agreed. "I've enjoyed my time here so much it hasn't seemed like work."

Lady Susan smiled. She gazed at her princess, and felt so glad to be with her.

The smile slipped from her face as she considered the lives this room might hold in the coming days. Wounded men. She never thought she would live to see war in her kingdom. Her heart was heavy as she considered how young her princes and princesses were to have to face such hard times as rulers. There had been times when she had wished for King Elyon's return, but now she felt desperate for it. How could these children lead their kingdom through a tragedy such as war?

Princess Margaret, who had been rearranging chairs to imagine where the beds might go, looked up from her task. She stopped and stared hard at Lady Susan. The lady had also stopped her work and was staring back at the young princess.

Princess Margaret spoke first.

"May I ask you a question?"

"Of course, Princess. You can ask me anything."

Princess Margaret paused for another moment as if trying to find the words.

Lady Susan tilted her head questioningly, her eyes remaining fixed on the young princess.

"Why can't women fight?"

Now it was Lady Susan who paused thoughtfully.

Princess Margaret sat down next to Lady Susan on a bench near a dark and cold fireplace.

"I wouldn't want to hurt anyone, it's just..."

Lady Susan waited for the princess to finish her thought.

"It's just that it seems like I should be doing something more."

Lady Susan shifted in her seat to be closer to the princess. "What you *are* doing for your people has great value."

"Yes," Margaret dragged out the word as she thought about it, "Yes, there is value in doing my part. But there is valor and bravery in battle! What does it take to fix up a house? In the scope of war, I feel *that* matters very little."

Lady Susan gently rested her age-worn hand on top of Princess Margaret's tiny one.

"My dear," the lady said, "We all have our roles; each one has a part to play. Not all of us can be soldiers and not all of us can be caregivers. For what would a wounded soldier do without his nurse and what would a nurse do without a patient?"

Lady Susan put her arm around Princess Margaret squeezing her shoulders and pulling her close. "If there is one thing I know about you, my precious princess, it's that you have plenty of bravery and valor without ever having to prove it on a battlefield. You will never cease to be useful to your people and your kingdom. Of that I am certain!"

6

Lady Dori drew her cloak up around her ears for warmth. She had just returned to Castle Grange as Prince Robert had instructed. She saw that Sir Edward and Sir Francis were already making preparations to leave for Falaise Bay. No doubt they had plans to lend their support and wisdom regarding the need for intervention with the Oblager or to further press their case that Prince Robert be crowned king as soon as possible.

"He says he will not return to be crowned at his castle while there may be a battle to fight," she explained to the men as they mounted their horses, ready to ride out.

They acknowledged her report with a nod and continued on their course, to reach Falaise Bay before the midday meal.

Lady Dori watched them go. She was thankful to be back at the castle. The Doyen had told her that Lady Susan was still shying away from most interactions with anyone else at Castle Grange. The woman who was usually bold and outspoken now walked about the grounds without a word and avoiding eye contact with anyone she came upon.

She would walk about, head bowed. When Lady Dori had inquired upon her return to the castle, Lady Claire said she had tried to talk with Lady Susan but the only person to have any success with that endeavor had been Princess Margaret. They had already left for the cottage in Colline.

"For who can refuse the young Princess Margaret?" Lady Claire had said with a wide smile.

And it was true.

Lady Dori thought about her own missteps and regrets over the recent months past. She remembered how her father had been so generous as to give her her inheritance, the Isle of Drepos, as a gift for the Oblager, in hopes that they would settle there. How she had tried to make the younger Oblager see the benefits of peace, the privilege of land and a place to call home. But Erik was stubborn and the sea was and always would be his home. He would not budge. Silas, the leader of the Oblager, and elder of the clan had graciously and gratefully accepted the island home. He was there now with the people loyal to him.

Lady Dori couldn't imagine what it would be like to have to take up arms against the men who had sat under their tent, who had been fed by them, men she herself had spoken to.

War is such a dark and desolate thing, she thought. *I wish... I hope it will not come to our land.*

7

The midday meal was to be presented in the tent high on the cliff above the port in Falaise Bay. But before the men at camp could settle down and eat their meal Prince Robert needed to check in with his brother.

On his way to search for Theodore, Robert was approached by one of their young guards. Elijah bowed before the prince. Then gesturing in the direction of where the guards had been running drills all morning, he said, "The men have been working hard."

"Very good."

As if he knew he was needed, Prince Theodore came toward them. He raised a hand in greeting and gave a half smile to the two standing near the fire. The day was turning cold and Theodore thought near the fire was the perfect place to be.

"I just met Sir Francis on the edge of camp," he said when he had finally reached them and was warming his hands by the fire. "Another dove has been sent in attempts to reach our father and I was wondering, what do you think about sending someone to try again to negotiate with Erik? Assuming he would talk?"

Prince Robert shook his head, "I think we should wait for the backup that is sure to come from Allia any day now."

"Is it?" Theodore asked his brother, barely waiting for him to finish his sentence. "How can you be sure Allia is sending aid? What if Samuel has trouble on the road? What if King Facile changes his mind about how friendly he's willing to be with Monde? It seems to me, nothing about Allia is certain. We are on our own, Robert."

Prince Robert sighed deeply. Why was Theodore always so argumentative? Or was he right? Should they be planning a strike rather than waiting. What were they waiting for? What was *he* waiting for? Was this just another instance where he was willing to wait for what he would consider a sure thing? Did he just want to wait for a way out of what seemed to be an inevitable battle at sea?

"No, They're baiting us," Prince Robert reasoned out loud, as much to himself as to anyone else. "They want us to take to the sea, leaving our port and our lands unprotected."

"Could Erik be so bold as to think he can still invade and pillage our kingdom even with his reduced numbers and with our guard on high-alert?" Theodore asked.

"He did take Lillian right from under us!" Robert reminded him. "It seems he is so bold."

Theodore nodded, conceding that point. Their enemy was wily and bold. It was hard to know what Erik was planning or what he would be willing to do to get what he wanted.

"I wish I knew what he wanted," Theodore thought aloud.

"Don't we all?" Robert agreed with his brother. "It would make this part of our job so much easier, wouldn't it?"

"If I may," Elijah spoke to both princes, bowing his head in respect. When he knew he had their attention he continued, "We know what Erik wants. He wants to preserve his way of life at sea and he wants to have his way with our kingdom."

With his anger sufficiently fueled Prince Theodore added, "And with our sister!"

The younger prince breathed heavily and turned to look at his older brother, the acting King of Monde, "We can't let him have his way!"

The conversation was halted as some of the men began bringing in provisions for their meal.

"We shall continue this discussion later," Prince Robert said to Elijah and Prince Theodore.

They did not discuss strategy over the meal and instead ate in silence.

After he had finished his meal, Prince Theodore returned to the training ground with Elijah. The young soldier was known to be skilled with the bow and arrow. He had suggested to Prince Theodore that the coordination skills the prince showed in the stunts he sometimes performed while riding Honor could be an indication of how well he could perform in archery. Prince Theodore had tried his hand at archery in the past, with very little thought or effort. He had different motivation to try it again now.

Elijah brought him out to the fields where the archers were training. With bow and arrow in hand Prince Theodore took his place in the row of men waiting their turn to shoot. It felt good to be out with the men. Theodore could feel their energy and excitement. They were all planning and preparing to take the fight to the Oblager should the need arise. He felt he was ready too.

He held the bow in his hands and positioned the arrow

against it. He steadied his left hand forward and drew back the bow and arrow with his right. The tension of the bow being stretched like that felt so good. Theodore felt strong with the tension held between his hands, the power of the arrow suspended and held back by the muscles in his arms and back. He focused hard, pulled up on the bow and shut one eye to better focus on the target straight ahead of him. Then, he released.

Thwack.

The arrow met its mark. Theodore's smile spread wide across his face. He was good at this and he enjoyed it. He liked the feeling of the tension and then the satisfying release. When it came time for battle, he knew this would be his weapon of choice.

8

Prince Theodore was simply impatient about the situation at hand. He had trained with the troops and found he was quite adept with a bow and arrow with very little training. Hand-eye coordination came naturally to him. This encouraged his determination to engage the Oblager in battle or at the very least to plan a rescue mission to get his sister back. He had started talking battle strategy as soon as the Doyen had arrived in camp.

"I think we should come up with a plan for Princess Lillian's rescue. We cannot allow her to spend another night on that ship!"

"We must exercise caution," Sir Edward said, following his prince toward the center of camp.

The young prince had wasted no time in initiating the conversation that was in line with his desires, but the wise older man knew that this was not a matter that would be easily resolved.

"Princess Lillian's safety is of utmost importance. This may mean we have to be patient and wait," Sir Edward cautioned.

"Be patient? And wait for what?" Prince Theodore urged. Then, in an attempt to be more agreeable he explained, "Of course my sister's safety is the most important thing and because of this I am convinced we must move quickly. God only knows what she must be suffering on that ship!"

Elijah, the guard who had been training all morning with Prince Theodore and the troops, joined them as they walked toward the tent to see Prince Robert. It was late afternoon and the guards were resting after their meal while the princes and Sir Logan were to meet with the Doyen. Sir Francis, who had not been slowed by conversation, was already sitting down to have his meal when Prince Theodore, Elijah and Sir Edward entered the tent.

"I must admit that I am conflicted regarding our next move," Prince Robert was saying to Sir Francis. Then he turned to the captain of his guard and asked, "Are you certain that Malaya is aboard one of the Oblager's ships?"

"I cannot be certain which ship she is on but she felt confident she would be able to board any one of their ships without incident," Sir Logan confirmed.

"And how confident are you in her?" Prince Robert pressed.

"I have absolute confidence in her abilities. If she said she could board a ship, I believe she will do it."

Prince Robert nodded.

The wind whipped through the tent, the snap of the fabric filling the silence.

"I believe engagement is the best course of action. We should not depend upon a spy we are unable to locate. We cannot risk the ship taking off in the night, taking our sister with it," Prince Theodore stood as he spoke loudly to be heard over the sounds of the struggle between wind and canvas. "We must show these rebels who is in charge, who is stronger. They must learn if they *dare* to enter into our kingdom they *will* submit."

"Prince Theodore," Sir Francis also stood, bowing low. He spoke softly so that all in the tent had to lean forward to hear his words, "your concern is warranted and the points you make are valid. However, if we were to engage the Oblager one of two things might happen: they would either flee, taking Princess Lillian with them. Or they would engage and we would be very limited in our offensive moves as we have no idea which ship holds the princess." The eldest Doyen nodded to Prince Robert before returning to his seat.

Prince Robert stood, finger tips massaging his temples as he considered what every one had to say.

"I appreciate your input, Sir Francis," Prince Theodore said, showing his respect for the wise man who had also counseled his father throughout his reign. "However, if we are not going to attack then we might consider planning a rescue mission. It does not seem wise or prudent to sit still and wait, giving the Oblager time to plot *their* move."

"Well, we are getting nowhere," Prince Robert sighed, running a hand through his hair. "Everyone involved has made excellent points. I know that you all have the well-being of not only Princess Lillian but also the entire Kingdom of Monde on your minds. I appreciate your input and we will continue our discussion but first, I must rest. Let us meet around the fire later this evening. I believe I shall have a fresh mind then."

Sir Logan ducked out of the tent and headed back to his men. Prince Theodore followed close behind him, determined to continue training with the soldiers.

Prince Theodore felt a hand on his arm.

"My Prince, could I speak with you a moment?" a man behind him said.

He turned around to see Elijah bowing before him.

"Elijah, what is it?"

"My Prince, if you don't mind, could we speak privately?"

They walked away from the tent. Once they were a significant distance and sure to be alone, Elijah continued.

"I have a plan, but I am not certain Prince Robert would support it."

"A plan for what?"

Elijah paused for a moment then admitted, "A plan to rescue Princess Lillian."

"Tell me!" Prince Theodore responded without hesitation. He was so excited at the thought that he had to remind himself to breathe.

Finally, he thought, *some action!*

The young soldier lowered his voice, leaned in toward the prince and said, "My cousin owns a small boat. He is a seasoned sailor and is not afraid of the wind and waves that winter brings. He would be ready to sail at your command. And I would be ready to go with him. We would sail to the Oblager ships, I would board them and find Princess Lillian. We could have her back safe on land by morning if all goes well."

The young man spoke with such confidence that it was difficult for Prince Theodore to try to think of the other side. What if the tiny vessel struck a rock before they even reached the ships? While the ships were not far from shore it was still a risk. Yes, a risk.

Prince Theodore stopped, taking the young man by the shoulders and looking him in the eye. "Is this a risk you and your cousin are willing to take?" he asked. "You know this will be a life or death mission."

The young man gave a nod. "Yes, I am determined. If it is your command, I will see it done."

Prince Theodore looked back toward Falaise Bay. This was so tempting. He bit his lip and tried to think calmly, rationally, but this is what he had been waiting for: a plan. How could he say no?

"See to it," he said, with as much confidence as the young soldier showed.

Elijah bowed low and ran off to fulfill his mission.

9

As evening fell across the Beaumere Sea yet again, Princess Lillian found it hard not to lose hope. Malaya had said it might take some time and the princess trusted that the young woman knew what she was talking about. Even so, Erik seemed to get angrier and louder with each passing hour and Lillian was thankful that for the most part he made her stay below deck in the cabin. It was warmer there and Lillian didn't feel as vulnerable or exposed when she was locked into her quarters. So when she was brought out onto the deck after dinner she told herself not to be anxious.

"You need to move around a bit. That's one of the rules of life at sea. You can't stand still. Moving around will keep you healthy and strong. Now," Erik instructed, waving his hand, "walk around."

Lillian looked around the ship. The men were not running around the deck busy with work as they had been during the daytime when she usually took her walks. There were a few men that were set to tasks but for the most part the men were either below deck or leaning against the railing drinking and eating. Those who were on deck watched as the princess walked slowly around them. After the first lap and feeling painfully awkward under the stares of the crew, she walked faster and hurried past the men, avoiding them altogether when she could by skirting around barrels or choosing the opposite side of the mast from where the sailors stood. Halfway through her third lap around the deck Princess Lillian heard a scuffling sound and loud voices. It sounded like there was a fight going on somewhere near to her. There was yelling and banging and within moments the fight broke out through a door and tumbled in a heap of bodies onto the deck. Two men and-

Princess Lillian let out an involuntary scream and immediately slapped a hand over her mouth.

Erik looked from the pile of people to the princess then back at the pile again.

"What is going on here?" he growled. This commotion did not help his already surly mood. "What are you doing?"

The second part he yelled, his voice echoing off the water. He growled at the trio still scuffling about on the floor.

"Get her up! Get her up!" One of the men was yelling.

"I'm trying!" the other yelled.

When they finally stood Malaya was being held firmly in the grip of two of the Oblager crew. She struggled against their grip. Her steely eyes were focused and her jaw set. The wind blew the hair from her face and there was no mistaking, it was the spy who had come to save her. Princess Lillian stood frozen in her tracks. She couldn't move, couldn't speak. She just stood, eyes wide, waiting to see what would happen to her ally.

"Who are you?" Erik roared, hopping down from his

perch and reaching the three people standing in the center of the deck now.

When Malaya didn't speak, Erik put his face inches from hers and shouted as loudly as he could, "I asked you a question!"

Princess Lillian flinched but Malaya didn't. She stood firm and even continued to wrestle against the grip of her captors.

Erik looked over at the princess, "This a friend of yours?"

He had motioned toward Malaya when he said it. Princess Lillian did not answer. She did not move. She wasn't sure what to do or how to help. She couldn't imagine how giving away the truth of Malaya's identity would help. But what would Erik do if he didn't get an answer to his question? Princess Lillian followed Malaya's lead and stood silent.

"I can tell from the look on your face, Princess, that this is one of yours."

Lillian shook her head slightly, imagining that if she acted like she didn't know the young woman then maybe Erik would leave her alone. She hoped this would save Malaya and that Erik wouldn't hurt her. But that seemed unreasonable. Erik was unreasonable, unmerciful. Princess Lillian began to shake uncontrollably. Standing still had allowed the cold of night to descend on her, and fear was weakening her muscles, causing her joints to become unreliable.

Erik turned back to look at Malaya. He grabbed her chin in his hand and said, "Who are you, girl?"

She still didn't speak.

"Well, if you won't tell me who you are then you are a stowaway and Oblager code says stowaways walk the plank.

'You can't pay for passage, you can't stay til port,' is what I always say."

He chuckled then and the men holding Malaya laughed with him. He stopped laughing as abruptly as he had started and nodded his head toward the side of the ship where a gang plank would be if they were docked at the port. The men wrestled Malaya to the side of the ship. She continued to look forward, keeping her chin up in resolution of her plight. Someone brought a rope and her hands were tied behind her back. She did not fight with them.

"Last chance, girl," Erik snarled. "You either tell me everything or off the side you go!"

Erik took another look over his shoulder at Princess Lillian. She stood still as a statue, jaw dropped open, struggling for breath, eyes wide. "Well, Princess?"

She couldn't speak. She tried to move her jaw. Her mouth was dry and she licked her lips to try to moisten them in an effort to speak. Should she scream? She looked past Erik to Malaya and they made eye contact. With the slightest movement of her head to one side Malaya's signal to the young princess was clear. Lillian understood that the brave and beautiful spy wanted her to do nothing.

They shoved Malaya to the edge of the deck, facing the darkness of night and forced her to step forward onto the short platform that led to nowhere. Two steps and then nothing but ocean.

Should she just tell Erik who the young woman was? Doing nothing didn't seem right. But it was hard to know what would be the right thing to do at this moment. Lillian watched as the men forced Malaya out toward the black darkness, inch by inch. The wind whipped her clothes around her and yet she stood tall and strong. A scream was rising up from within and stuck in the back of the princess's throat. Just as the air in her gut met the sound she held in her mouth, there was a loud-

Splash.

Princess Lillian released her scream and her knees buckled beneath her. Two of the crew who were standing nearest to the princess ran to her, picked her up by each arm and hauled her to her cabin. Princess Lillian's breath came fast now. She looked back, craning her neck to try to see. See what, she wasn't sure. She listened hard for any splashing. Any sounds of swimming or motion. Any signs of life. But she saw nothing. She heard nothing. Then cries filled the air and Princess Lillian realized they were coming from her. She tried to control them but could only somewhat stifle her sobs. She could not believe what had just happened. She could not believe what they had just done. *Malaya.*

Moments later, or perhaps hours, the men let go of Lillian's arms and she dropped to the floor. When she came to her senses at last she saw she was in her dark cabin. She breathed rapidly as she heard the sound of the cabin door being locked behind her. Only then did she allow herself to cry aloud once more.

10

The conversation around the fire later that evening did not prove to provide any further direction. Prince Theodore tried to remain calm and quiet about his own secret plan, the one that Elijah had presented to him, the plan that was more than likely at this very moment under way.

"And what do you think?" Prince Robert said to Prince Theodore. "You've been quiet. That's very unlike you. What is your view?"

Prince Robert didn't take his eyes off of his brother but continued to stare at him as if trying to read his expression or his mind.

"My thoughts have not changed since earlier today, brother. My thoughts are toward action. And the sooner the better. The Oblager cannot be allowed to strategize for themselves. We must have the upper hand!"

A couple of those gathered around the fire nodded in agreement but Theodore noticed his brother did not look convinced. Robert was usually the cautious one, so this did not necessarily surprise him.

"We will see what tomorrow brings," Prince Robert said with a tone of finality. He stood and wrapped his cloak tighter around him. "I want to give Prince Samuel the time he needs to reach King Facile and to get the ships from Allia launched before we call an attack that may, in the end, not even be necessary."

"A show of force with the extra ships should take care of those young rebels," Sir Francis agreed.

"Extra ships and perhaps a crowned king?" Sir Edward added.

The large man spoke meekly, which was so unlike him, Sir Francis almost laughed. Surprisingly, Prince Robert did not even smile. He stood frozen, considering the words his Doyen had spoken.

There was a moment of silence as they waited for the young prince to respond. Prince Theodore assumed his brother would relent now but then again-

"What was that?" Prince Theodore, turning toward the noise he had heard, jumped up from his seat by the fire.

There was a scuffle behind them and then into the light stepped one of the guards holding a short man who was struggling to break free form the larger man's grip.

"Silas," Prince Robert recognized him first and stepped forward into the light of the fire.

The elder Oblager, who was previously thought to be on the Isle of Drepos, stepped forward and quickly bowed before Prince Robert. The white hairs in the man's beard and on his head glistened in the fire light and he knelt on the ground before the acting king of Monde.

"Your Grace," he said, then standing again, "It is good to see you."

"To what do we owe the pleasure of this visit, Silas?" Prince Robert asked sitting back down.

"I see Erik has not yet left your shores," he began, taking a seat when offered and leaning forward, elbows on knees.

"Indeed he has not," Prince Robert hesitated but then confided, "and he has taken our sister, Princess Lillian, aboard his ship."

Silas gasped and sat upright. He looked to Prince Theodore who nodded in confirmation. "I had no idea he would go to such lengths..."

"What is he doing out there?" Prince Theodore tried to remain calm as he questioned the elder leader of the Oblager.

"That is what I came to speak to you about. I sailed here this afternoon to talk with you, to tell you-"

"Tell us what?" Prince Robert interrupted.

Theodore looked at his brother in surprise. It was so unlike Robert to be impatient.

"To tell you that Erik will not leave until he has done what he came here to do. He and his men are rough and have the desire and stamina to wait you out."

"What about the other ship?" Prince Theodore asked. "Will it be coming? Is that what he's waiting for?"

"That is precisely what he is waiting for," Silas confirmed quickly. "They will bring supplies and more men. That ship will come unless an act of God sinks it."

"That is what we shall pray for then," Prince Theodore said.

"Theodore!" Robert spoke sharply to his brother, "Show some grace."

In a soft tone he said, "Silas, you know that if there is a way to retrieve my sister and to watch Erik sail away without any of us coming to harm, that is the path I will take."

Silas nodded.

"What must we do to see that outcome?"

Silas sat silently chewing at his bottom lip. He stared into the fire, the flames illuminating his wide eyes.

"Your Grace," he said finally, turning slowly toward Prince Robert, "I am afraid that may not be possible. Erik will not relent. It may come to the point of battle. One thing I do know: if he has taken your sister he intends to marry her. He will protect her as the treasure she is. No harm will come to her by his hands. You will not have to fear for her in battle, as long as your strategy does not include sinking ships."

Again, silence fell over the group. The wind howled as it blew up the cliffs and whipped through the nearby tent.

"Are you hungry?" Prince Robert asked Silas, then to one of the guards near the tent, "Please get this man something to eat."

Then without another word Prince Robert stood, nodded to Silas and walked away to his tent, the captain of the guard close behind him.

11

At Castle Grange that morning plans were already underway and preparations were being made to decorate the dining hall for William's birthday the next day. True to her word Lady Susan had created scented candles that reminded Margaret of both the smell and the color of the moss on the forest floor, an earthy green. She knew William would love it. Princess Margaret and Lady Susan worked away in the dining hall that morning cleaning and preparing for the rest of the decorations to be brought in. It was the day before Prince William's birthday and while everyone was living on edge, feeling as though their nerves were on pins and needles, together now they tried to muster a sense of celebration in honor of the youngest prince.

Sir Nelson was bringing in bouquets of winter folliage and arranging them around the room. The banner bearing the House of Rosh family crest that Princess Margaret had commissioned Lady Dori to restore just over a month ago was still in its place high on the stone wall of the dining hall. Lady Dori brought in more banners and pillows to soften the room and add to the charm for the birthday celebration. The smell of baking wafted up the stairs, down the long corridor and into the room where they worked. It smelled heavenly. Soon the cakes and breads created by Lady Claire would be placed on the table for Prince William to discover in the morning. This was all tradition and it was something that Margaret loved to participate in, whether the planner or the honored participant. Birthdays were great celebrations in her home. The night before a birthday everyone would gather in the dining hall, except the guest of honor, and they would clean and decorate for the celebration that was sure to come the next day. Accordingly, William was not in the room but was out making a last check in at the dovecote.

Princess Margaret stopped what she was doing and looked around the room. In that moment of silence, her heart sank. While all the decorations were there, her family was not. Her father was off on a mission in only-God-knew-where, if he was alive at all. Samuel was in Allia looking for help. Theodore was either at the armory or at the bay with Robert. And Lillian...

Margaret ran from the room, down the stairs and out the front door into the night. The cold air slapped at her cheeks as she ran making them red. She didn't know it at first but as her tears began to freeze on her face she realized she was crying. She kept running until she came to the stables and ducked inside. The air was a bit warmer there, at least it didn't hurt to breathe. She found a cloak hanging by the door and wrapped it around herself, pulling the hood up over her head for extra warmth.

"My girl," Delight said, stepping forward. "Why are you crying?"

Margaret tried to stop herself, tried to take a deep breath

but couldn't. She was crying uncontrollably and ran to Delight, wrapping her arms around the horse's neck.

"I'm so sad," the young princess said. "I'm sad and I'm worried. Poor Lillian is out there on the Oblager ship and... And tomorrow is William's birthday and... And we have no idea where Father is..."

Margaret allowed herself to cry, she didn't know how long. Delight stood still, nuzzling against her and breathing steadily to soothe her. Eventually, Margaret was able to breathe deeply, her sobbing stopped and so did the tears. Her heart felt heavy and as did her arms, which she dropped to her sides. She stood up straight and stepped away from Delight for a moment.

"I'm better now," she said. "I need to go to Falaise Bay and see what is happening. I need to know."

Delight did not speak.

"If you go, I'm going with you," came a voice from the stable doors.

Margaret turned around to see William standing there.

"I want to go to the bay too. I want to know what is happening. I think we both should go and we should go tonight," he said to his sister, putting his arms around her in a tight hug when he was close enough to do so.

"Are you sure?" Margaret asked.

"I'm positive!"

"But tomorrow is your birthday. Won't you miss waking up and going into the dining hall for your birthday surprises?"

"It wouldn't be the same without my family," Prince William spoke steadily. "I'm determined to get down to Falaise Bay and see what's happening. What do you think, Allegiance?"

The young prince's Sage Cheval nodded his approval and stomped a hoof in agreement.

"It's set then. Margaret, you need to go change and I'll go to the kitchen and grab some food. Let's meet back here as soon as we can and then we will be off."

The two youngest royal children in the Kingdom of Monde ran back into Castle Grange and set about their plan. It wasn't long before they were saddled and riding high on their Sage Cheval, headed toward what they knew might soon be the battle front.

12

"Ship on the horizon!" A voice called throughout camp early the next morning.

"Three of them!"

One of the guards had gone out early in the morning, training his spyglass out to sea and had returned with the report.

Everyone was still in their tents. At the sound of the soldier's cry Robert and Theodore looked at one another and jumped up from their cots. They pulled on their boots and cloaks as they ran from the tent. As soon as they reached the cliff's edge Prince Robert took the spyglass being handed to him. He extended it and peered through it to the horizon.

"Samuel has done it!" he exclaimed, handing the spyglass to Theodore so he could take a look.

"It's hard to see the flag flying from the masthead," Theodore said, reserving his excitement for such a time as he was certain the ships headed their way were friendly ones.

Prince Robert snatched the spyglass out of his brother's hand and gave a disappointed groan.

"Samuel must have done it. There are three ships on the horizon and as far as we know the Oblager only left one ship in reserve. Silas's ships are safely moored off the cost of Drepos."

Theodore knew the leader of the Oblager, Silas, his crew and their families were eager to make their new life on the Isle of Drepos work. They had received the gift from Lady Dori. The garden island had been in her family for centuries and now it was a true extension of the Kingdom of Monde and the Oblager who had pledged friendship and fealty to the throne of Monde were living there peacefully even now.

"The Oblager reserved only one ship *we know of*," Theodore specified for his brother. "That does not mean there aren't more. Erik may have planned to overthrow Silas even before they reached our shores. I won't be satisfied until I can see those flags."

The younger brother took back the spyglass from his older brother, the would-be king, and said, "Let's have a peek at what is happening aboard the Oblager ships. If they're busy on those decks I bet you anything they are preparing to launch their attack on us."

"Or preparing to defend themselves against the ships of Allia," Robert suggested, pausing for a moment to consider his brother's words and finding himself much less confident in his resolve that those were indeed friendly ships.

"What are they doing down there?"

"Oh they look very busy," Theodore said, trying to hide his emotion. "I told you. I don't believe those are friendly ships at all. They seem to be coming from the west more so than the south."

"Any ship coming into the Bay would have to come up and around, appearing to have 'come from the west'... Theodore, you're making me nervous."

"Robert," Theodore handed the spyglass back but did not let it go. He turned to face his brother and said quietly, "I think we need to be prepared for an attack. If those indeed are friendly ships then we have done no harm and will be armed to aid in the battle. If we do nothing, depending on the victory of our allies, then we may very well find ourselves in trouble if the ships prove to be with the Oblager."

Prince Robert nodded.

"If I may," Sir Logan said, bowing before the two princes. He had been standing quietly but felt he needed to interject now.

"Of course," Prince Robert said, "What are you thinking, Sir Logan?"

"I too believe that whether friend or foe, we should be ready for battle either way. Prince Theodore is right: if the ships are friendly they may need our ground forces yet. The weak nautical forces we have are standing by, but I'm not quite sure what two ships will do if those three at sea are reinforcements for the Oblager. If they are not friendly, well, then, we shall be ready to meet them."

"Very well then," Prince Robert said. "Assemble the troops!"

Prince Theodore took the spyglass and went to the edge of the cliff looking out. He had something else he was looking for. Someone else. Where was he? Elijah had said he would be back by morning, with the princess. But there was no sign of either a small vessel out on the water, nor the two guards who had sailed out the night before. Theodore paced back and forth, scouring the shoreline and the area around the ships anchored just off the port in the bay.

"C'mon, Elijah. Where are you?" Theodore's question was carried by the wind and back toward camp.

"What did you say?" Robert said from behind him.

Theodore jumped, surprised his brother had followed him.

"You scared me! I thought you were inspecting the men."

"Sorry, Theodore. It wasn't my intention to scare you. You were talking to yourself..."

Robert paused then noticed the look of concern on his brother's face.

"What is it? Why are you so upset?"

"I'm not upset," Theodore argued, but he knew it was useless to try to fool his brother. "Okay, I *am* concerned."

"About what?" Robert pressed.

"I'll tell you, but you're not going to like it."

"What is it?" Robert stepped closer to his brother, worry now wrinkling his own brow before even having the answer to his question.

"Prince Robert!" A guard was yelling and running toward them on the path along the cliff. "Prince Robert!"

The man bowed low when he reached the two princes. He held something in his hand, a gray cloak with something wrapped in it.

"This was found on the shore this morning. It came in with the tide along with the wreckage of a vessel of some kind."

The man handed the cloak to Prince Robert. He unwrapped it and inside was a sword.

"Oh no," Prince Theodore whispered, putting his hand

over his mouth and looking back out over the water. "Oh no."

"It's Elijah's sword," the guard explained to Prince Robert. The prince turned to his brother, "What is it, Theodore? What does this mean?"

Theodore dropped to his knees in front of his brother and hung his head.

"He thought it would work," Theodore said quietly.

"What? Who thought what would work?" Robert said, trying to show his brother patience but clearly running short of it, "Theodore, tell me now!"

Prince Theodore got up on his feet and looked his brother in the face.

"Last night, after we had talked about...waiting..." his voice trailed off. "Last night, Elijah came to me along with his cousin. They said they had access to a boat. They wanted to sail out to the Oblager ships and find the princess, rescue her and bring her back with them by morning."

"What?" Prince Robert turned toward the man who had brought the sword and the news of the wreckage, "Were there any bodies found? Was there anything that would indicate that Princess Lillian was aboard the small ship?"

Theodore's eyes grew wide and he grabbed Robert's arm as they waited for the answer.

"No, my prince. No bodies and nothing to indicate the princess was aboard. We will keep an eye out today and let you know if anyone or anything comes ashore."

Prince Robert thanked the man, barely able to speak and nodded to dismiss him back to his post.

He looked at Theodore, trying not to allow his emotions to get the better of him. Between clenched teeth he said, "Did it not occur to you that this plan would be very risky?

That our sister could have drowned in the course of this attempted rescue?"

Theodore shook his head, fighting back the tears.

"Now two of our men are missing or worse yet, dead..." he looked away from his brother, "Theodore, would you slow down and think? If you, if they had waited just a few more hours..." Prince Robert was clearly frustrated now, "Did you not think Samuel would be successful? We have ships coming to our aid as we speak."

Theodore stared at the ground. He couldn't even look at his brother.

"It's such a waste. A tragedy." Robert let out a long deep sigh.

Prince Theodore pinched the bridge of his nose to stop the tears. He took a deep breath and looked Robert in the eye. He nodded his agreement. He couldn't handle being under the critical stare of his brother any longer. He knew Robert had a reason to be angry, and he was right, that rescue mission had put Lillian in danger. He had not thought of it before. Now, he would have to suffer the wait along with everyone else. Why had he been so quick to risk the lives of Elijah and his cousin? Why had he not thought more about the danger they were putting themselves in, and potentially Lillian herself?

With a slight bow Theodore turned from his brother and walked, nearly ran, away from him. He was going to join the ranks of men as they armed themselves. Theodore knew what he could do. He decided no matter who was on those ships, he would be ready, armed with his bow and arrow. He would fight right alongside the soldiers of the Kingdom of Monde.

13

From high in the crow's nest a voice yelled down to the men on deck. From her position on the floor near her door where she had fallen, or had been dropped, the night before Princess Lillian could hear the shout.

"Ships to the south-east!"

She sat up. She could feel the tears crusted to her cheeks. Her body was aching from the cold and from her night spent on the floor. After she had seen Malaya disappear off the edge of the ship, heard the splash as she fell into the water, Lillian had been unable to stand. Even now, the young princess could not believe what she had witnessed the night before. She wanted to cry even now as she recalled the events on the deck. The spy, her hero, falling into darkness and then she herself had fallen onto the deck. She had been dragged back to her room. She had not even had the strength to stand. In the light of the new day that streamed in through the cabin window, the events of the night before seemed like a dream. Malaya was gone. She had died trying to save her. She had-

The call came again from the deck, "Three ships to the south-east!"

Princess Lillian got up and moved as quickly as she could with stiff joints to look out her window. She wondered if the stern side of the ship was facing south-east and was glad to see that indeed it was.

"Are you coming to save me?" she asked out loud, her voice cracking.

The door of the cabin swung open and in came the same two men who had been bringing her all of her meals.

"Breakfast, Princess," the rough Oblager said, smacking her tray down on the table.

The sound made Lillian jump and she turned to face the men, pulling her shawl tight in front of her as if she were holding a shield.

The younger man gently set down a pitcher and a tin cup he had tucked under his arm then picked up the items that had bounced off the plate and put them back on it.

Princess Lillian realized the voice calling out the watch had sounded excited, and not in the good way; the man on look out was worried. She decided to try out her theory.

"Those aren't Oblager ships," the princess stated boldly to the men who stood staring at her.

The angry man's sneer deepened the lines in his forehead. The kind young man's eyes went wide.

"I'm sure you can tell that from here," she continued, hoping one of them would say something to confirm her suspicions.

"You know nothing about it," the older man growled as he turned to leave.

Princess Lillian raised her chin and gathered all the confidence within her and said boldly, "I would imagine those ships are coming for me!"

Concern was settling over the younger man's face and Princess Lillian knew that the hot headed Oblager would erupt with the truth of the situation, she just had to wait for it.

"Shut your mouth!" the angry Oblager had taken two steps toward the princess before the younger man grabbed hold of his arm to stop him from getting closer.

"Let go," he growled, wrenching his arm out of the young man's grip. Then he spat, "Who cares about the imagination of a little girl?"

With that he lumbered from the room.

The young man apologized to the princess under his breath then bowed to her slightly before leaving. As soon as the door was shut behind them and she heard the snap of the lock, Lillian spun around to look back out at the ships.

If they weren't Oblager ships, she wondered, who were they?

Prince Robert stood by, the spyglass to his eye.

"The flag looks nothing like the Oblager flag. In fact, I have never seen anything like this ship before."

If the Doyen had been present he would have asked one of those wise men, but as it was they had returned to the castle, first in hopes of preparing a crowning ceremony, but also in effort to maintain some semblance of normalcy in celebrating Prince William's eleventh birthday.

"Let me take a look," the boy next to Robert said.

Prince Robert looked down to see his youngest brother, William, standing by his side.

"What are you doing here?" He smiled wide. "Come here!" He said and reached for his baby brother.

Prince Robert hugged William close. "It's your birthday! You're missing you morning celebration in the great hall."

"We couldn't imagine being able to truly celebrate without all of our family together," Princess Margaret said, coming up alongside her brothers who were standing at the edge of the cliff.

Prince Robert drew her into the hug and kissed the top of her head. "Won't our guardians at the castle be disappointed when they wake up to find you two gone."

"They'll be mad," Princess Margaret agreed.

"But, like Margaret said, we wanted to be with you and Theodore today. We have heard nothing from you since Lillian was taken and we needed to know what was happening here," William explained.

Margaret nodded her head and both younger siblings looked to their oldest brother for answers.

"I wish I had something to tell you," Robert began slowly. "Malaya is expected to be aboard one of the ships in hopes of protecting Lillian, perhaps even aiding in her rescue. Our guard Elijah had plans of his own to attempt to rescue our sister, but it seems he may have met his end on the water last night."

Margaret gasped and clapped a hand over her mouth in shock.

"There are three ships on the horizon, coming from the south east. They could be the ships from Allia, the ships we sent Samuel to ask of King Facile, but..."

Margaret grabbed the spyglass from her brother's hand and looked out to sea. The three ships were easily seen by the naked eye, but more details could be discerned through the spyglass. "I don't recognize those flags."

She handed the spyglass to William. He looked for a

while, hoping the wind would take up one of the flags and expose its full image.

"Hm. I don't recognize it either. And those ships look rather unique. I'm not sure I've seen anything quite like those vessels in our waters before."

"Good point, William," Robert agreed. "I hadn't given it much thought, but now that you say so... They certainly don't look like they're from Allia as I had hoped..."

"So I see you have men in place along the cliff and along the shore. Are they preparing for a land battle?" Margaret retrieved the spyglass to take a look along the shore at the soldiers.

Robert sighed. "We are preparing for any eventuality. It seems that Erik would have fled by now were those ships not Oblager vessels, and yet, there he sits in our harbor."

"From anything Lady Susan and Lady Dori have said, it seems like Erik is bullheaded enough to stand his ground and see his goal is achieved," Margaret said.

William nodded in agreement with his sister. "True. I for one am convinced those are *not* Oblager ships. But if not Oblager, and not Allia, then who?"

———————

14

There were men lined up all along the edge of the cliff. Some of the archers were on the highest ground, while those trained in sword combat were below nearer to the trail down, ready to charge the port at a moment's notice. There were men lined up along the shore, hidden behind barrels, posts and anything they could use as a shield. Prince Theodore stood among the archers in town, nearest the docks. He had been training with them intensely for days. It wasn't his first time training with a bow and arrow, but while training here in camp, now during this most important time, he had come to learn how skilled he was with the instruments of warfare he had chosen. Sir Logan had even remarked at his skills.

The Doyen had surprised the young royals by returning to camp later that morning. When it was discovered that their guest of honor for the birthday celebration that was supposed to take place in the great hall that very morning had left the castle, they had left too. Sir Francis was standing near Prince Robert now.

"Well, Sir Francis," the young prince said when the elder

gentleman had joined him, "are you disappointed that we are not in the midst of a crowning ceremony at this moment? Or even a birthday celebration?"

He gave the prince a half smile and a nod.

"I must say, given what it seems we are facing right now, I too would rather we were at Castle Grange in the midst of either celebration. Though crowning me king would be like admitting-" he stopped short and turned to look at Sir Francis. "I don't think I'm ready to admit that my father very well may be... *Dead.*"

They stood in silence for a moment. Then Prince Robert stepped forward, looking out over the sea. "And so, here we are. I am for peace. But it seems no matter what I say they are for war. Taking Lillian was the last straw!"

He swept his hand in front of him as if to touch the tips of the sails of all of the ships in the bay.

Sir Francis put a reassuring hand on the young man's shoulder. "No matter what they say or do, when the time comes you will be ready."

Prince Robert nodded solemnly. He looked at all of the men lined up to his right and to his left. He looked down along the shore. The men were identifiable only by the color of their hair or the symbols on their cloaks. But Robert could see Theodore down at the docks, standing at the ready with his arrow balanced in the arch of his bow.

Theodore stood as still as stone. He could feel his muscles twitch from the tension. A bead of sweat rolled down his temple even as the cool breeze of early winter chilled his skin. He tried to hold the bow and arrow steady, squinting out toward the bay, toward the ship he was certain held his sister captive. Theodore had been waiting for this moment, waiting for action. He fought against the urge to release his arrow. He could see movement on the decks of the ships that were anchored no more than 50 yards from where he stood. He kept his eyes trained on the shape of a man, someone he thought he had recognized from their days of negotiations in the tent, when the Kingdom of Monde had tried to broker peace but the Oblager had demanded their own way, the way of conflict and even all-out war.

Theodore felt the hair on the back of his neck rise. The three ships coming, still too far in the distance to identify filled him with dread. For some reason he could not bring himself to believe that those were the ships from Allia. It just didn't seem right. Something didn't feel right to him at all.

"If they want war," Prince Theodore breathed, "they'll get it."

"Pardon me, sire?" The archer to his left asked, hearing only that his prince had spoken but not understanding his words.

"Nothing to worry about," Prince Theodore reassured the young man with the wrinkled brow. His focus disrupted, Theodore took the opportunity to reposition himself. He rolled his shoulders back to release the tension there and drew up his bow. Setting his jaw, he took aim at the man at the helm of the largest Oblager ship. He breathed steadily, waiting. He wanted to be ready.

"Steady men," Sir Logan came up from behind walking the line and encouraging his men to wait for the signal from on top of the ridge where Prince Robert stood. "Wait."

It had been decided they would hold their positions until they could determine the identity of the ships heading straight for them. Friend or foe? That was the question everyone was asking about those ships but Theodore felt that it was foolish to ask questions, foolish to wait. If they launched an attack now and the ships were friendly, they would only come to join the fight. But if they were foe, then the second wave of soldiers on the cliff would provide the assistance needed at that point. This waiting though...

Theodore could hear his breath inside his head. The world around him seemed to fade away as he focused on the man standing on the deck of the ship that held Lillian. His sweet sister. He would do anything for his sister. Anything. But would he *kill*? Could he kill? His breathing grew more rapid and his muscles tensed again, his body stiff from holding the bow and the arrow drawn back.

There was a crash behind the line as a soldier dropped his shield with a clang.

Theodore jumped and without warning his arrow was released.

"Hold your fire!" Sir Logan shouted again at the sight of the arrow that had been sent sailing over the water toward the boat.

Theodore blinked hard, almost unable to believe his eyes. The arrow flew over the water, reached the deck and met its mark. The man who had been under the heat of Theodore's stare fell out of sight. The other crew members flew to where he had fallen, all except for one man, who stood staring back toward shore, either unmoved by the incident or incensed by it.

Theodore swallowed hard.

What had he just done?

15

Murmurs went up and down the line of the archers gathered along the shore. Whispers of shock and surprise could be heard being passed from man to man.

Prince Theodore stood still. Unable to look at anyone. Unable to move. What had he done? What had just happened? He couldn't believe it. Had he just killed a man?

"He killed him," one of the men whispered.

"Prince Theodore made the first strike," another said.

"Our fearless leader!"

"What a shot!"

While the men seemed to admire the young prince and his marksmanship, Theodore was numb. He dropped the bow and it clattered against the rocks beneath him. He looked down as if surprised by the sound.

Sir Logan came up beside him and touched his shoulder, which made the prince jump.

"Your Grace?" The soldier looked at the young prince's pale face. Sir Logan drew closer to Prince Theodore, ready to hold him up if need be. Concern wrinkled his brow and he kept his gaze on his prince.

The cold wind off the water picked up again and slapped the men's faces. Theodore blocked his face with his arm.

He had killed a man. He didn't deserve shelter or comfort or victory. He had taken a man's life and all he could think was that he deserved for his life to be taken too. Prince Theodore looked Sir Logan in the eye and then without a word broke formation, running from the line of archers in search of Honor. He had to get to his Sage Cheval. He had to get out, had to leave.

"Prince Theodore!" Sir Logan called after him. But there was no reply.

Theodore found Honor and was in his saddle within a moment.

"Go as quickly as you can to Castle Grange!"

"What has happened?" Honor asked.

But Prince Theodore did not reply. He wasn't sure he could say it out loud. If Honor ever knew... if the only ones who ever knew were those who had seen it happen, that would still be too much.

Theodore felt confused, tangled up in his thoughts. Dangerous thoughts. Or perhaps *selfless* thoughts?

What if I were to take the Book of Enchantments? Perhaps I could find a way to bring the man back to life?

He urged Honor to move faster, thoughtlessly clicking his heels against the horse's flanks.

Honor tried again.

"What has happened, my boy?" He asked.

Again he was met with silence. The only sound that could be heard was the pounding of hooves on the wooded path leading to Castle Grange.

If the spell found in the Book of Enchantments had hidden the castle for all of those years there must be a way to bring the dead back to life within its pages, Theodore thought. *And if there is a way to bring him back, I must find it. I could not live the rest of my life as a ... murderer.*

"I'm sure there's more to the story than what you can contrive, my boy," Honor said, having gained some sense of the thoughts that troubled his young man.

Theodore paused in his mind for a moment and looked down at his wise companion. Maybe he *should* confide in Honor? He could just tell him everything about Elijah, his secret plan and the arrow that had struck the enemy... Maybe he would know what to do? Theodore allowed himself to think for a moment that perhaps the situation wasn't so bad after all. Perhaps *he* wasn't bad. No. Theodore shook his head. It was too much to speak of and so he continued on in silence.

When they were finally safe inside the gates of Castle Grange, Theodore jumped down from his saddle and left Honor alone in the courtyard. He ran into the castle without a word.

"What have you gotten yourself into, my boy?" Honor wondered out loud, looking toward the castle.

He did not move but stood where Theodore had left him, waiting.

"Where is Prince Theodore?" Prince Robert asked when he had joined the archers on the line along the shore.

"He has... fled," Sir Logan explained.

"Fled?" Prince Robert questioned, hands on hips, brow wrinkled in confusion. "What do you mean, *he fled*?"

Sir Logan took Prince Robert aside and spoke quietly,

"Your Grace, your brother shot an arrow at the ship Freedom and killed a man on deck."

"He - he - killed a man?" Prince Robert stammered, looking back over his shoulder toward the ridge, toward the road that would eventually lead home.

He shook his head as if shaking off the reality of what he had just heard. He couldn't make sense of it and wasn't sure he should allow himself the time to consider it now. There was a battle threatening to break loose at any moment. He had to stay sharp, focused.

"Where did Prince Theodore run to?" Prince Robert asked Sir Logan quietly.

"He seemed to be looking for Honor, but I cannot be sure."

The young prince nodded and looked back toward the road once again. Should he go after his brother? What was there to be said or done in the situation? He imagined Theodore must be torn up by what had happened to Elijah, not to mention the shot he had taken, but he was needed here. Theodore would have to wait.

"The mysterious ships will reach those of the Oblager in less than an hour by my estimation," Prince Robert said, tending to the task at hand. "We must be ready."

Sir Logan nodded and began his trek up and down the line of archers.

"Steady men," he said. "Be ready."

The mysterious ships drew nearer to the shore and reached the Oblager ships in almost the exact amount of time Prince Robert had predicted.

Prince Robert and Sir Logan made their way back up to the ridge and watched the approach of the mystery ships with great interest. The approaching ships angled themselves as if to surround the ships of the Oblager. One ship in particular, the largest in the fleet, positioned itself alongside the Freedom. Once high above the bay, Prince Robert pulled out his spyglass and could see the men aboard the Freedom scrambling, most of them brandishing swords as they ran to get into formation.

"They are no friends of the Oblager!" Prince Robert called out to the line of men.

Then, he hailed Sir Logan. The captain was at his side in an instant.

"They are not friends of the Oblager, but are they friends of Monde?" Prince Robert asked handing the spyglass to the soldier who took it and stared through it for a time. With a sigh Sir Logan shook his head.

"I'm sorry to say I don't recognize the flag and there is not one crew member on deck of those mystery ships. I can't imagine what they are doing."

Behind them there was a galloping of horses hooves breaking into the quiet. Prince Robert and Sir Logan spun around to see Prince Samuel and his squire Caleb riding into camp. They ran over to greet the riders who were already dismounting. Samuel touched his forehead to Endurance's and held there for a moment. Caleb tied Lark up to a nearby post and led him to some fresh hay.

"Welcome back, Samuel!" Robert said, pulling his younger brother into a big bear hug.

"It's so good to see you, Prince Samuel!" Sir Logan said with a bow. Then to Caleb he said, "Welcome back. Your father will be glad to see you!"

"It's good to be back," Prince Samuel said. "I have so much to tell you! And King Facile is most certainly our friend. He has agreed to send three ships from Allia. They should be arriving any time now.'

Prince Samuel nodded for Caleb to go and find his father as soon as he had secured his horse.

"My dear brother, I do believe Allia's ships may be in our bay as we speak," Robert said.

Prince Samuel raised an eyebrow and looked at his older brother, "Let me see those ships. I don't know *how* they could've beaten us here. I would have expected them this time tomorrow."

It was time to go back to the shoreline and prepare for action. Once there Prince Robert pulled out the spyglass and handed it to Prince Samuel who quickly put it to use. After only a moment, Samuel looked at Robert, his face telling Robert what he thought he already knew.

"Those most certainly are not the ships that were sent from Allia," Samuel confirmed.

Sir Logan took the spyglass and looked out, watching as the mystery ships drew ever closer. The question still remained: if the ships were not from Allia, then where had they come from? Were they friend or foe to the Kingdom of Monde?

Prince Samuel took the spyglass back and surveyed the Oblager ships. He wasn't sure what he was looking for. Maybe he hoped to see a sign that Lillian was safe, at least as safe as she could be when a captive aboard an enemy ship. But there was no sign of her.

"It looks as though the Oblager are preparing their defenses," Samuel said, handing the spyglass back to Robert. "If they're planning to defend themselves against the mystery ships, what does that mean for us?"

"We should know very soon," Sir Logan said, "And we will be ready."

16

Princess Margaret and Prince William had remained in the tent as Robert had instructed when he and his men had left to go down to the shore. Margaret insisted that they get back in the saddle directly and head down to the port below. But William just shook his head and helped himself to some of the food left out from what must have been a late breakfast.

"I need to eat," he said, chewing on a piece of bread he had dipped in a cup of milk.

He stepped to the edge of the tent looking out into the sea.

"Hey," he said slowly, talking with his mouth full and not caring about manners. "You need to see this..."

Margaret first looked at her brother with frustration but then her jaw dropped open when she looked out over the water to see the three ships sailing into port at last. The ships were almost close enough to see the people on deck now, yet not close enough to identify them without the aid of the spyglass.

"I wish I could identify those flags," William was saying, mouth finally empty, as Margaret looked around for a spyglass. She wanted a closer look.

When she couldn't find what she was looking for she returned to her lookout and shielded her eyes from the sun. Even the color of the mystery flags was different from that of the Oblager.

"I truly believe Samuel did it," Margaret nodded, gaining energy and excitement with this determination. "He did it! He made it to Allia and they have sent their ships! It is done! Lillian is saved! *We* are saved!"

"Margaret," William spoke slowly and softly, "It doesn't make sense. Those are not the flags of Allia. And look at the shape of those ships. I've never seen anything like them before."

Margaret sighed in resignation. Then, seeing the flash of silver from on board the deck of one of the foreign ships, she knew weapons were being drawn.

"But, they do not look like they are friends of the Oblager!"

Suddenly, a shout hit the shore, carried across the water from the largest foreign ship. Prince Robert snapped the spyglass open and looked through it to see a group of young men leaping from that ship onto the deck of the Freedom. The ship had pulled up alongside the Oblager before Robert had time to realize it. He could see men as they leapt aboard the Freedom, shouting and wielding their weapons. The weapons looked like long spears or swords but some seemed to be made from wood and had feathers attached at their handle. The group of foreign soldiers handled their weapons skillfully and fought their way across the deck of the Oblager ship.

The Oblager men stood by, short swords at the ready, yet unused, as they seemed too shocked by the strange sight to move. Erik could be seen animated, running from place to place shouting at his men to move, to fight. But he was one of a few who were actually using their swords.

Within moments, the other two ships had come up alongside those of the Oblager and the same thing seemed to be happening aboard each ship.

Prince Robert stood amazed, watching through the spyglass as their enemy was being vanquished. But what would the conquerors expect in return for this victory?

"What's happening out there?" Prince Samuel asked, unable to see a thing without the help of a looking glass.

Without a word Robert handed the spyglass to his brother and turned away.

He ran down the line to his captain, "Sir Logan, should we send our own fleet out now?"

"That would confuse things," Sir Logan said. "We should wait and see what their next move may be."

"It's their next move I'm concerned about," Prince Robert explained.

They walked back to where Samuel stood, and the young prince handed the spyglass to Sir Logan so that he could assess the situation.

Sir Logan took a moment to survey the decks of each ship. He saw what his prince had seen: the Oblager men scattered and confused and the men from the mysterious ships jumping onto the decks and skillfully fighting the Oblager. He noted that the men from the foreign ships seemed to be decorated for battle. Some wore masks, others wore paint on bare chests. The bellows that came from each man as he jumped onto the Oblager ships to attack could be heard over the water and on the shore.

Prince Robert took the spyglass back into his hand, raised it to his eye and trained it on the ship that held Erik and his men, and it was assumed, Princess Lillian. He saw that the deck had been overtaken by the men from the foreign ship. He watched as all of Erik's men, the rebellious Oblager, sunk to there knees on the deck of the ship. What he saw next, made his jaw drop open and took the breath from his lungs. His arms went limp. The spyglass fell from his hands and dropped to the rocks near his feet with a clank.

Sir Logan startled at the sound of it and looked down at the spyglass then up at the face of Prince Robert. His face was as white as a ghost.

"What is it, your Grace?" Sir Logan asked, touching the prince's arm and looking him in the eye.

Prince Robert said nothing. He did not move.

"Robert?" Samuel searched his brother's face once more. He stood as still as stone.

Prince Samuel moved quickly and snatched up the spyglass. He looked to the ships to try to find what it was that Robert had seen. He scanned the deck of one ship, then another. At last he saw it and had to catch his own breath. Barely able to speak he choked out, "Father?"

At that word, Sir Logan forgot all manners and propriety, grabbing the spyglass from Prince Samuel's limp hands and looked out to the Oblager ship Freedom. Once this was confirmed he couldn't hold it in.

"The- King!" Sir Logan stammered then yelled, first out to sea then he turned and yelled again, "The King!"

All along the line of soldiers each man stood, craning their necks, trying to get a better look.

Sir Logan pointed to the ship and continued to shout, "The King! King Elyon! He lives!"

17

P rincess Lillian had watched the ships come ever closer from the relative safety of her cabin. She had seen the ships sail up alongside the Oblager and now she could hear the commotion from on deck.

She was being rescued. She just knew it.

She banged on the door, "Help me! Help! I'm in here!"

She screamed at the top of her lungs but there was so much noise outside. The shouts of the crew, the clashing of steel and the pounding of boots could more than drown out her cries.

Lillian laid down flat on the floor and tried to see under her door. The guard who had been standing his post at her door was still there. She could see his feet shuffling from side to side. Then, he fell. He fell right in front of the door and she could no longer see anything but his body blocking her way. He was still and she knew he was probably dead.

She waited hoping to hear more or to learn something of what was happening outside her door. In moments, she saw from the bottom of the door that the guard's body was being dragged away and she heard the sound of the key in the lock. She hurried away from the door looking around her for something to grab that she could defend herself with but the only thing available in the room was a chair, so she gripped its sides.

Suddenly, the door flew open with a loud bang and before her stood-

"Father!"

Princess Lillian let out a cry. She slapped a hand over her mouth and blinked away tears. Tears of joy she thought, but she couldn't be certain. It was so much to take in. She wanted to believe it was her father who stood in the doorway but she wasn't sure she could believe her own eyes. He looked much the same as she remembered him, if not a little more wrinkled in the skin, skin that was tanned from prolonged exposure to the sun. She could also see gray in his hair at his temples and around his ears. But he still looked large and strong to her. He was the most beautiful sight she had seen in a long time. She hadn't expected her rescue to be at the hands of her father and she found herself breathless at the sight of him. She could not wait to be near him, to touch him and hug him and yet, somehow she was frozen in place.

He held out his arms to her and she broke free from her trance. They ran toward one another until they met in a tight embrace. Princess Lillian ran right into her father's open arms. She wrapped her arms around his waist and buried her head in his chest. She inhaled the scent of him and squeezed her eyes shut trying to capture the moment in her heart and mind, a memory to keep forever. He showered her head with kisses, held her cheeks in his large hands and gently kissed her forehead. Finally, he pushed her away from him, holding her by the shoulders at arms length.

"Let me look at you," he said in a raspy voice. "You have grown, my beautiful girl."

Lillian smiled and blushed. She realized she had been such a small girl when he had left for Estrea two years earlier. "My daughter, my Lillian."

He knelt down to look at her closely.

"Are you alright?" He was searching her from head to toe,

She nodded breathlessly, "Father...You're...You're alive! I..."

Suddenly, a young man Princess Lillian had never seen before ran into the room. He had a weapon in his hands and he lowered it, bowing his head to her as he scanned the cabin with his eyes then turned his back to her to look behind him and behind the door to ensure they were not being watched.

"Princess Lillian," he acknowledged as he bowed his head to her.

She nodded to him then looked to her father. This was no citizen of Monde. He had dark skin and dark features, which made the white of his teeth sparkle. The whites of his eyes and the soft blue of them stood out in stark contrast to his brown skin. There was no one in her kingdom who looked like this.

"This is Gavin," King Elyon explained. "He and his mother saved my life. They are with me now to retrieve you and to rid Monde of the Oblager. Come now."

King Elyon put Lillian behind him as they went toward the door, instructing Gavin to keep hold of her as they went.

Gavin acknowledged the king then gave Lillian a reas-suring smile and grasped her hand in his. It was warm from the fight, which felt good since Lillian hadn't felt warm in days. He was strong and he pulled her along, all the while glancing back at her with a smile or nod to reassure her.

King Elyon forged their way forward and Gavin kept looking behind for any Oblager soldier that might be attempting to sneak up on them.

Princess Lillian followed her father out of the cabin and toward the stairs, but before they could ascend, their escape route was blocked. Two men jumped out from the lower deck and drew their swords. King Elyon quickly pushed Lillian and Gavin further behind him.

A sharp sound rang through the air as the king pulled his sword from its sheath and growled at the men.

From behind two more men came upon Gavin and he forced Lillian to stand between him and her father. He had a spear to defend them with and he began to rock back and forth, twirling it deftly in one hand, then in the other. The Oblager watched as he spun his weapon in front of them. One of the men lunged forward. He jabbed into the air with his sword. He was unable to get close enough to actually do anything. This gave Gavin the second he needed. With a swipe of his spear he swept the first man's feet out from under him, sending him toppling to the floor.

The other man advanced on the foreigner, but his knife got caught in the twirling spear. The knife was wrenched from his hand and flung across the deck. The Oblager who still held a sword attacked from another direction. Princess Lillian watched as Gavin held his spear tightly, spun around ending up behind the man so quickly that before anyone knew it the long spear of the foreigner was held to the Oblager's neck. He gasped for air and held onto the long handle of the spear with both hands. He struggled to pull free, but was held fast. The other Oblager scrambled for his knife, grabbed it up and ran the opposite direction, leaving his comrade to fend for himself.

"Leave," Gavin snarled into the ear of the man he held close.

The man couldn't respond. He could barely breathe.

"I will release you and you will go and jump off of this ship."

The Oblager nodded. Then he was released with such force that he fell to his hands and knees choking. As soon as he was able he jumped to his feet and ran up the stairs, out of sight.

On the other side King Elyon was wielding his sword with one hand. The Oblager who were fighting him with their short swords seemed smaller than the king in every way possible. Lillian was surprised to see they were continuing their attempts to attack him. He shoved them back with every clash of the sword. They were getting tired, Lillian could see it.

"Surrender!" King Elyon instructed finally.

He lunged at the smaller of the two men, locking swords with him and twisting until the man's sword was wrenched from his hand and fell to the floor with a clatter. The unarmed man run away, leaving his comrade to fend for himself.

The Oblager kept on and after a couple more jabs of his sword, that only resulted in the king's simple parlay of the attack, his sword was finally torn from his grip and toppled to the ground. King Elyon's sword was at his back in a moment and he pushed the Oblager onto the deck.

When they reached the top of the stairs Princess Lillian froze for a moment. She did not understand what she was seeing. Gavin looked at her and waited patiently for the scene before her to make sense. There were many more warriors on board the ships, deftly fighting the Oblager into submission. She realized she recognized none of the men she saw who were fighting for her father, fighting to rescue her. They all fought with spears and were dressed much differently than she was used to, most of them not wearing the thick clothing required for the cold weather of late autumn.

Perhaps they had never been to Monde and had no idea how cold it would be, Lillian thought, then reprimanded herself for focusing on such things in the midst of a battle. She kept moving. Now that he had been returned to her, she did not want to be too far away from her father.

King Elyon walked out onto the deck of the Oblager's ship. With his feet planted firmly, he stood his ground. His hands were clenched into fists that pressed onto each of his hips. Lillian saw that he was standing very near to Erik and it seemed they had been engaged in a very intense conversation. Erik looked overheated and overwrought. His cheeks were almost as red as his hair. Most of his men lay wounded and the rest were scurrying around in chaos.

The roar of the ocean mingled with the shouts of the Oblager and the battle cries of the foreign warriors suddenly seemed deafening to Princess Lillian who stood staring straight ahead, waiting to see what her father, the King, would do next. Then she heard him shout.

"I don't want to have to kill you," he bellowed over the roar of wind and waves, "but that's exactly what I'll do if you do not return my daughter to me and leave these shores. I promise you, I will not stop until each one of you lies breathless on the deck of this ship!"

Erik stood as still as a statue. As if he hadn't heard the words that were bellowed by the King of Monde. He seemed to be surveying his options, looking back at the other ships, as if willing one of her Father's ships to be his own. But they were not. The three ships that had sailed in were from a foreign land and Erik was outnumbered. He would not win this fight. He knew this.

Princess Lillian watched as he clenched his jaw. Then in a slow, deliberate movement he knelt on his left knee and offered his sword to King Elyon. The deck of the Freedom became quiet and still. The men stopped running about and focused their attention on their leader who was bowing in surrender to the King of Monde. With his head slightly bowed Erik did not move. He stayed in this position until the king came over and took the Oblager's sword from his outstretched hands. All across the deck men began kneeling on one knee, dropping their weapons and bowing their heads in the same way that they saw their leader had done.

King Elyon stood tall over the men bowed before him and raised the Oblager sword over his head, signaling to the other two ships that their leader had surrendered. Lillian could see the fighting on board the other ships slowly come to an end.

Princess Lillian let go of Gavin's warm hand that had once again grabbed hers. She felt an exhilaration that she could not explain. She looked at all the men bowed before her father and she moved quickly across the deck to stand next to him. When he saw her beside him, a smile broke across his face.

He handed the Oblager's sword to his eldest daughter, then turning toward the men bowed before him said. "Because my daughter has been returned to me unharmed, I will show you mercy and allow you to return to your life at sea."

King Elyon's voice seemed to start deep within his abdomen then burst forth across the deck. Lillian could both hear and feel the rumble of his words as he held her tightly against him with one hand.

Taking the Oblager sword from her, he held it up above his head.

"I will not use your sword against you. Go now and do not return to this land, for the kindness I have shown you here today will expire if ever I see your faces in my kingdom again!"

With a nod to his men, King Elyon pulled Lillian back toward the ship he had sailed in on. No word was needed. King Elyon's men moved back toward their own ship. Gavin was soon by her side and once again took her hand. She didn't want to leave her father's side, but he nodded his command without a word to her as well. She knew he meant that she should go, so she did. Gavin smiled at her as they went.

She gave a weak smile back, all of a sudden feeling very tired. She let Gavin lead her onto the deck of the foreign ship, her father's ship. It looked different from those of the Oblager. It was much friendlier than the ships suited for war that she had spent the last few days on. Gavin, still holding her hand, led Princess Lillian to a cabin that was not hidden below, but that was situated in the middle of the ship's deck.

Lillian turned to look behind her and saw her father's men filing off of the Oblager ships all the while Erik was yelling to his men to ready their ships for sailing. There was much activity aboard all of the ships and it made Lillian feel a bit dizzy. She must have swayed where she stood because Gavin was quickly beside her to hold her up with a gentle hand around her waist to support her. She thanked him with a nod and a smile as he helped her sit down on some cushions so she could rest.

Lillian would have looked around her to gather all the

details of her surroundings if she had not been so exhausted. She would have seen the kind faced woman with long dark hair sitting on her own cushions just a few feet away from her. Perhaps she would have noticed the young girl and two boys sitting next to the woman as well. As it was, Lillian found now that she was more comfortable and warm than she had been in days it was difficult to keep her eyes open. Her eyelids were very heavy and soon, they fell. And soon, she was fast asleep.

18

P rincess Margaret and Prince William arrived at the docks and saw that Endurance was there. They hopped down from Delight and Allegiance and ran to hug Endurance around his neck. The Sage Cheval neighed lightly, enjoying the affection from the royal children.

"Samuel is down by the docks," Endurance explained. "He will be very happy to see you two!"

"We are so glad to see you safely back in Monde," Margaret said before parting with William in the lead, heading down toward the docks.

Robert saw his siblings and at first was annoyed that they had foolishly entered into what potentially could become the frontlines of an all-out war. But then he loosened a bit when he realized, this is exactly what he should have expected them to do.

Samuel followed his brother's stare and when he saw Margaret and William walking toward them he closed the distance, sprinting to get to them as quickly he could. He wrapped them both into a hug and couldn't wait to tell them the news.

"I adore you, brother and sister and what I am about to tell you will make you so happy…"

He was smiling from ear to ear. It looked like it hurt. He was smiling and not talking.

"Well?" Margaret couldn't stand it any more. "What? What do you have to tell us?"

"Father," Samuel said simply, "Father has come home!"

Margaret ran as fast as she could to the line of men at the docks. She found Robert and Sir Logan, both with the same dreamy smiles on their faces that Samuel had.

"Is it true?" she asked. "Is Father on one of those ships? Has he come home?"

She was almost in tears, unable to believe this was true.

William ran up beside her in time to hear Sir Logan say, "Yes, Your Grace. It is true. Your father has saved Princess Lillian and has come home!"

William and Margaret, who by this time was blubbering through her tears, hugged one another tightly with joy.

"Father is home!" William shouted. "Woohoo!"

Robert ran to join the hug and kissed the top of Margaret's head, rubbing a hand over one of her cheeks to dry the tears. "He is home, baby sister. Don't cry!"

She smiled up at him and nodded.

"I want to see him!" the young princess cried.

Robert handed her the spyglass and she looked out to where her brother directed her. She scanned the deck of the ship and could see men kneeling down.

"Lillian!" Margaret screamed and jumped up and down as she continued to look out at the ships. "I see Lillian!"

And a moment later: "There's Father! Wow. He looks different."

"Let me see," William demanded, taking the spyglass from her and looking out.

It was indeed his father and something within him warmed. His heart swelled. Never in his life had he been happier to see anyone or anything.

"I can't *wait* to hug him," he said rapturously.

"Can I see that again," Margaret asked, taking the spyglass back without waiting for his answer.

She looked out at the ship to see Lillian being escorted to the cabin on deck by a young man with dark features. She looked back to see her father shouting instructions to warriors that obviously answered to him. When he spoke, they listened. As her father's men seemed to withdraw from the Oblager ships, Margaret saw something that confused her. A woman with long dark hair came out of the cabin Lillian had entered not long before. She had a determined look on her face and seemed to be helping give orders to the men that were returning to the deck of her father's ship. The young woman stood beside King Elyor as he continued to direct his men. Then the strangest thing happened. Margaret saw her father put an arm around the young woman and kiss her forehead. The young woman smiled up at him and put a hand to her large, round belly.

Slowly, Margaret lowered the spyglass, her brow furrowed and smile gone from her face.

"What's the matter?" William asked, taking the spyglass from her and looking back out at the ship.

Apparently, he did not see what Margaret had seen because all he said was, "It looks like father is in charge out there!"

"I'm not sure *what* it looks like out there," Margaret said under her breath.

19

The urgency, the desire for action that Theodore had struggled against out at the port had now changed into something else. He *had* to get away. The port, the Oblager, even Lillian, seemed miles away. The first sign of the Oblager ships that had been only days ago now seemed like years in the past and the tension between his people and theirs seemed a blur in his memory. The conflict within his heart and mind was at the forefront of his attention. All Prince Theodore could see in his mind's eye was the man standing on the deck of the ship then falling. The man had fallen out of sight.

Theodore could still feel the arrow leaving the bow as he had held it. But he couldn't remember making the decision to release the arrow. He had done it. And he had taken a life. He *had* to get away. He wouldn't be able to live with himself if his actions had ruined the chances to negotiate for Lillian's return? What if it had started an all-out war? It would be all his fault. He had to try to make it right. In his mind he saw the large leather bound book sitting on its shelf. The thick volume, ancient and powerful. The Book of Enchantments. If there were any way to make it right, any way to bring the dead man back, it would be in that book. He had seen firsthand the power that it held within its pages. He himself had witnessed his entire castle disappear, hidden from the sight of all but those who lived there. He could see the shimmering haze of the spell that had been cast over these castle walls. He knew the enchantments worked and he would use them for his purposes now. He needed to make this right. He ran up the stairs to the top of the tower, to the solid wooden door that led to the rooms that held the book. He opened it without knocking and to his relief they, the Doyen, were not at their desks.

He ran to the back room and followed with his eyes along the top row of the bookshelf until he saw what he was looking for. He moved the ladder that stood against the stone wall and placed it near the volume he was trying to reach. Quickly he climbed up and grabbed for the book. His hand slipped a bit and he pulled it back with a cry. Blood dripped from his finger and he put it in his mouth to stop the bleeding. He had forgotten that about this book. It was powerful and it was treacherous. He would have to be more careful. He took the leather gloves that were folded over his belt and put them on, then cautiously he gripped the dark green spine of the book and pulled it from the shelf. He tucked it firmly under his arm before descending the ladder.

He sighed with relief as his feet once again touched the floor. He hugged the volume tight under his arm and all but ran from the Doyen's study to his own room. As fast as he could he began throwing things on his bed that he knew he would want to pack. The Book of Enchantments first placed gently there, then a change of clothes, some parchment and his winter cloak. He put his lighter cloak on him and raised the hood. He wasn't sure where he was headed except that he felt he should go north. The Wild West Wood wasn't the wisest option, the sea was to the east and Samuel was to the south. So, north it would be.

Before exiting into the courtyard Theodore stopped in the kitchen to put some food into his pack. He grabbed a handful of nuts and popped them into his mouth as he packed. He drank some water and left out the back of the castle. He was relieved he had not seen anyone and assumed that most everyone from the castle would probably be at Falaise Bay except for the contingent of guards that had been assigned a post along the castle walls. He was surprised he hadn't seen either Margaret or William but was also thankful of that fact.

When Prince Theodore rounded the castle and made his way to the front courtyard he was surprised to see Honor standing exactly where he had left him.

The young prince approached his Cheval slowly, almost timidly. Honor did not speak. The wise horse knew there was nothing that could be said to help his young man. Not yet. Theodore would have to ask before Honor would say a thing.

Together they walked out of the gates of Castle Grange in silence. Once on the road Theodore hopped into the saddle. Without a word, the two companions began what they both knew would be a long journey. Instead of a leisurely walk, Theodore pressed into Honor and the Cheval's pace quickened. Once they had reached Valea and the road forked, they took it north, past Colline, through Ploin, and on. When they passed by the falls Theodore realized with added regret that it was William's birthday.

What a terrible day for William, he thought. *This is a dreadful day for a birthday.*

He realized he hadn't even noticed if the great hall had been decorated as was tradition for all birthday celebrations. The castle had seemed entirely empty. He imagined how that might make William feel so lonely. But maybe he was with everyone else at the port now, ready to do his part to retrieve Princess Lillian or to protect the kingdom. Theodore was sure of one thing: he knew the noble men and women his father had enlisted to care for them in his absence were brave and fiercely loyal to the house of Rosh. They would lose life or limb to save his sister, to guard their kingdom. Theodore was certain no matter what mess he had unleashed on that Oblager ship, that they would do all they could to make it right again.

That is why I must do all I can to make this right... His thoughts drifted. He wasn't sure he would be able to make it right. *At least I should stay away so I don't do any more damage.*

Honor could sense the desperation in his young man. He knew Theodore was hurting, but also knew he would have to wait for his young man to open the door to him. This was not something Honor could force his way into. So they rode on in silence. Night began to fall and the temperature dropped as they continued north. Before the first star shone in the sky snow began to fall, lightly at first and then the flakes grew in size. Thankfully, the moon was full and the light it shone reflected off of the snow that now covered the ground. Theodore wished he could wait for it, but with the sun gone he was cold, so he pulled out his winter cloak and wrapped it around him. They had made better time than he had imagined.

He began to wonder about Lillian and the troops at Falaise Bay. What had happened after he had left? He tried to shake off those thoughts and to focus on the immediate matters, such as, where were they going to be able to rest for the night?

Honor remained silent. He would let his young man figure things out for himself.

20

P rince Robert called to his soldiers. Sir Logan commanded them to line up along the shore and to the docks, swords drawn in allegiance, preparing for the king's arrival. The royal children on shore watched as a small vessel was lowered from the deck of their father's ship. It was carrying him, Lillian and several others who had been aboard his ship. All the while, the ships of the Oblager were heading out to sea, away from the Kingdom of Monde. Upon his defeat, Erik had wasted no time in setting sail. Once King Elyon knew the Oblager were leaving, he set about preparing to go ashore, preparing for his homecoming.

A dove had been sent from the great tent on the hill to Castle Grange as soon as the king's presence was known. A message was written to let all within its walls know of the king's return and encourage them to come to the shore to greet him. Hours seemed like days as Princes Robert, Samuel, William and Princess Margaret waited along the docks for their father to arrive and for Lillian to be safely returned to them.

As they waited, the Doyen joined them, with smiles spread across their faces and nervous energy causing them to shift their weight from foot to foot while standing at attention. Soon after the Doyen's arrival Sir Nelson and Ladies Susan, Dori and Claire also arrived. They were breathless from the ride and had clearly left the castle as soon as they had received the dove. Night was falling now and everyone waited in eager anticipation for the boats from the great ships in the bay to arrive. They were waiting for King Elyon's return.

21

Mercifully, the moon was high and bright in the night sky as the Kingdom of Monde awaited the return of their king. The small vessels carrying precious cargo were rowed ever-closer to the docks in Falaise Bay. It was so quiet that the lapping of the water against the wooden boards could be heard along with the knocking of the paddles against the ships.

Minutes seemed like hours and time had never moved more slowly. Until, at last, after an eternity, Princess Margaret thought, the ships reached the docks one by one and were tied into place. Margaret found she couldn't stand still. She was bouncing. And yet... She was waiting to learn more about the beautiful young woman she had seen her father kiss. It had been so long and there were so many questions. Margaret could hardly stand it. Her three brothers were standing side-by-side, standing at attention waiting for the King's arrival and their sister's safe return. Prince Robert stood as tall as he could with Sir Logan at his left hand. Everyone stood breathless, waiting.

King Elyon was the first to put his foot on his kingdom's

soil. He was holding Princess Lillian's hand on one side, and the dark haired young woman's hand on the other. When they had made their way off of the dock and onto solid ground, King Elyon let go of Princess Lillian's hand, knelt down on one knee, kissed his own hand and touched it to the earth. No one spoke. No one moved. With a wide smile the king looked up, taking in the view of all of those waiting at attention, waiting for him.

The night was so quiet and still until at last the king's voice broke the silence.

"My children!" King Elyon bellowed standing up and running to his children. Lillian ran too. There was so much laughter and so many tears. The hugs and the kisses and "I love you's" and "I missed you's" were exchanged and continued for sometime.

Robert held tightly to Lillian, more relieved than he could have imagined he would be by having her safely returned.

"I was so worried I would make the wrong move and you would be lost." he admitted to her as they hugged.

"You did well, Robert. I only regret that Malaya was found..." Lillian's voice trailed off and she hugged Robert even tighter.

King Elyon took each one of his children's faces in both of his hands to study them, each in turn. After exploring Samuel's face the king stopped abruptly.

"Where is Theodore?"

Everyone looked at one another and finally Robert stepped forward.

"He..." Robert began but wasn't sure how to finish, wasn't sure what to say.

Sir Logan stepped forward and bowed deeply from the waist.

"If I might?" he said, looking at Prince Robert to gain his consent.

Prince Robert nodded and the captain of the king's guard continued, "Prince Theodore ran away after killing a man with his arrow aboard the Oblager ship."

King Elyon looked confused and shook his head. "We left no man dead on board any of the Oblager ships. There were no deaths. Plenty of injuries, but no one has met their Maker this day."

Sir Logan and Prince Robert looked at one another in shock.

Prince Samuel turned to Lady Susan and asked, "Didn't Prince Theodore return to the Castle? Did you not see him there?"

The lady shook her head, "I did not see him."

The others who had come from the castle confirmed that they too were unaware of Prince Theodore's presence, if he had been at the castle at all.

"He was visibly shaken by what he thought he had done," Sir Logan explained.

"Well, we will certainly find him when we return to Castle Grange," Sir Francis stated with clear confidence.

It was resolved that the happy family would return to the castle as soon as possible to reunite with Theodore there.

King Elyon turned toward the party he had brought with him from the ships. He smiled at them, drawing the woman Princess Margaret was most curious about, closer to him. Looking back at his children he said, "Children, I would like to introduce you to my wife, Queen Luca."

"Wife?" Princess Margaret said quietly, to herself more than anyone else.

"She brings with her the children of her land that she

has adopted: Gavin, Anna and Noah," the king continued his introductions.

Lillian smiled at Gavin with recognition and gratitude, explaining to her siblings, "Gavin helped in the battle with the Oblager."

Queen Luca smiled and gently rubbed her large belly. King Elyon moved closer and put a protective arm around her shoulders and said, "We have also brought the next prince of Monde with us!"

Then king and queen laughed together as if sharing a joke.

"Or perhaps the next princess," Queen Luca reminded.

Princes Robert, Samuel and William stepped forward to acknowledge each of the new family members in turn. They saved Queen Luca for last.

Robert bowed before her, took her hand and kissed it. She smiled gently down at him, lifting him up by his arm and drawing him into a hug.

Lillian stepped forward to join in and soon all were hugging and talking with one another about the journey's they had all taken to arrive together at that place.

All were joined together except Margaret. She stood back, her father eyeing her from the center of the talkative group. She stood with her arms crossed and one brow arched.

"Too bad Theodore isn't here for all of this," she said loudly enough to be heard over the conversations taking place just a few feet from where she stood.

Everyone fell silent. It was a long silence as everyone waited to see if King Elyon would say something in response to his youngest daughter. But he did not. He simply nodded to her and looked about him, the moon illuminating his tear stained cheeks. His tears had been freely flowing almost as soon as his arms had wrapped his first child into them.

King Elyon walked over to Margaret and pulled her into a strong embrace. He brought her over to the group so that all were standing close, holding onto each other. With their long-lost father at the center of the group, they watched the ships of the Oblager fade into the darkness of night.

All at once a light snow began to fall. Prince William looked up and caught a snowflake on his tongue. He looked over to see his father smiling at him.

The king pulled his youngest son into a warm embrace and said, "Happy birthday, William!"

THANK YOU FOR READING
THE KING'S KINDNESS!

**If you enjoyed it, please help other people find this
book by:**

1. Writing an Amazon review.
2. Sharing the free read link at the beginning of this book!
3. Signing up for my new releases email so you can find out
about any giveaways or sales, as well as when the next book
is available!
Also, please visit and share: www.sarahfenlonfalk.com

Now, keep reading for a sneak peak of
The Good Prince,
Book 6 in the Sage Cheval Series!

THE GOOD PRINCE

BOOK 6 IN THE SAGE CHEVAL SERIES

*After accidentally letting his arrow fly and seeing an enemy
soldier fall, Prince Theodore has fled his home. With the
Book of Enchantments in hand the young prince hopes he
can bring the fallen soldier back to life, to correct his mistake
and free himself from shame. Will Prince Theodore find the
miracle he seeks in the Kingdom of Monde's north country?
Find out in Book 6 of The Sage Cheval Series!*

ACKNOWLEDGMENTS

First words of gratitude must go to my mom and dad, Susan and Gary Fenlon, who always told me I could and should write books for young readers. Thanks guys!

To my husband Pete, who was the first person in my adult life to call me "a writer".

A special thanks to Jon Jorgenson, for his YouTube 7 Minute Sermon series on the Fruits of the Spirit, which inspired the theme for each book in The Sage Cheval Series. I return to these videos when I get "stuck" while writing. Thank you, Jon! Keep up the good work!

And to my excellent proofreader, Kate Schlueter, for being willing to share her gifts and talents to make each book better: I thank you!

Finally, a very special thanks to my children Bobby, Ted, Sam and Will and to my nieces, Lillian and Margaret, for always asking for bedtime stories. And to my newest nephew, James for adding to the inspiration!

ABOUT THE AUTHOR

Sarah Fenlon Falk loves sunshine, dark chocolate, playing cards, days at the beach and writing! She lives in Chicagoland with her husband, four sons and therapy dog named Molly.

All of Sarah's books (and more!) can be found at sarah-fenlonfalk.com or most anywhere you shop for books!